DARK CASTLE
PRESS

First published in 2017

www.emmanuelledemaupassant.com

No AI programs were used in the creation of this book or associated audiobook

FIRST PUBLICATION

Highland Pursuits first appeared in shorter form in the charity anthology *Because Beards,* with all proceeds benefiting the Movember Foundation (supporting treatment of, and research into, men's health issues).

CONTENTS

HIGHLAND PURSUITS

BY EMMANUELLE DE MAUPASSANT

GLOSSARY

bairn - child
haud yer wheesht - be quiet!
wee - little

CHARACTER LIST - LONDON

Ophelia Finchingfield - our reluctant debutante
Pudding - Ophelia's cairn terrier
Sir Peter Finchingfield - father to Ophelia
Lady Daphne Finchingfield - mother to Ophelia, daughter of Lord and Lady MacKintoch

CHARACTER LIST - SCOTLAND

CASTLE RESIDENTS - UPSTAIRS

Lady Morag MacKintoch - grandmother to Ophelia and mother to
Lady Daphne
Aphrodite - Morag's Pekinese
Lord Angus MacKintoch - late husband to Morag
Edward (Teddy) MacKintoch - late son to Morag and Angus
Ebenezer McLean - brother to Morag
Lady Constance Devonly - old friend of Morag and Angus
Hamish Munro - nephew to Constance, working as manager for the
Kintochlochie Estate
Braveheart - Hamish's wolfhound

CHARACTER LIST - SCOTLAND

CASTLE RESIDENTS - DOWNSTAIRS

Mr. Haddock - butler
Mrs. Beesby - cook and housekeeper
McFinn - footman
Lyle - stable lad
Una - scullery maid
Jennet - kitchen maid
Nessa and **Maggie** - housemaids
Mary - lady's maid to Morag and to Constance

CHARACTER LIST - SCOTLAND

GUESTS AT CASTLE KINTOCHLOCHIE

Comte Guillaume de Montefiore - a French aristocrat
Felicité - step-sister to the Comte
Launcelot Horatio Buffington - an artist
Enid Ellingmore - author of sensational romantic fiction
Colonel Faversham - a dreadful old buffer
Rex - the Colonel's labrador
Ranulph Van Kloeper - a Hollywood director, and old flame of
Morag's
Loretta Van Kloeper - fourth wife to Ranulph, a former showgirl
Baronet Charles Chippington (Chips)
another of Morag's old flames
Peregrine Belton - a young man with a passion for motoring
Misses Evelyn and Alice Craigmore - lively spinsters of Aberdeen
Reverend McAdam
Lord and Lady Faucett-Plumbly

1

BANISHED

IN THE BACK OF A TAXI, IN THE SUMMER OF 1928, OPHELIA Finchingfield first realized her views on the wedded state.

It might have been the awkward, overly lubricated kiss, or the inept grope upon her breast that brought the revelation. Perhaps it was the conviction that her suitor lacked the brooding depth of a Heathcliff or a Rochester.

Whatever the substance behind her discovery, she accordingly turned down an offer of marriage from Percival Huntley-Withington who, at the tender age of twenty-two, had recently succeeded his father as Earl of Woldershire.

This so incensed her mother (the opinion of her father was of no matter) that Ophelia was placed on the next overnight sleeper to Scotland, to stay with her grandmother until she saw sense.

If Lady Finchingfield could overlook the Earl's mother braying with laughter in the manner of a horse, then Ophelia could put up with marriage to a man lacking sex appeal. In fact, thought Lady Finchingfield, the less pizzazz on that front the better. In her experience, less appealing husbands were rather easier to manage.

Unceremoniously banished from the social whirl of London, Ophelia reclined upon her bunk, rocked by the rhythm of the Scotch

Express to Inverness, accompanied by the warm snuffling creature that was her beloved Pudding.

She had insisted that where she go, her Cairn terrier follow.

Ophelia had never met Lady Morag MacKintoch but she feared her grandmother feeding her nothing but bread and water (physically and sexually) until she relented and threw herself back upon her mother's mercy.

Cabbage too. Ophelia shuddered. *No doubt, there'll be endless cabbage, and spinach, cooked for hours and spooned liberally onto the plate. The servants will have been thoroughly trained in the over-boiling of vegetables, and the very walls will be impregnated with the smell of Brussels sprouts.*

This sorry contemplation inspired her to extract her Cadbury's Milk Tray, hastily purchased at King's Cross station for such a possible crisis. Pudding sniffed hopefully as Ophelia tore the seal and chose a strawberry crème.

There had been boiled cod with egg sauce in the buffet car soon after departure, but Ophelia hadn't been able to face it. The honey sponge pudding to follow hadn't been bad.

'Not for you, little thing! It would only make you ill.' Ophelia popped the confection whole into her mouth and pulled back the edge of the curtain to see where they might be. Of course, it was too dark to tell. They hadn't reached Crewe yet, and Scotland was still a way off. As if by magic, she'd meet the dawn there, the train having done all the hard work through the night.

London would be at least five hundred miles away, or something like that. Geography had never been her strong point, although she wasn't without a few grey cells, and a reasonable amount of general knowledge shared between them.

To her mother's irritation, Ophelia had insisted on delaying her 'Season' until she'd finished her studies in art history at Girton College, Cambridge. In this, Ophelia was supported wholeheartedly by her father, who saw no reason for a modern girl to be without education.

Nonetheless, for the preceding year, Lady Finchingfield had been preparing for what she viewed as the true days of import in her daughter's life.

The summer had been spent in Paris attending the Louvre, the Philharmonie de Paris, and the Palais Garnier and, to Ophelia's joy, her mother had conceded that they should both visit the renowned Antoine in the Galleries Lafayette, to have their hair styled *a la mode*, in the boyish manner.

In matters of fashion, Lady Finchingfield could not bear to lag behind, and she emerged with a sleek bob. Ophelia, who in all things was more unruly, found that her curls refused to sit demurely, even under the expert hands of Monsieur Antoine. The hair springing wildly about her dainty face heightened her wide-set, violet eyes and her mother was unable to hide her dismay, but the cut gave Ophelia great satisfaction. Not only would it be easier to wash, but it well-matched her mischievous attitude. The overall effect was delightfully impish.

They'd been outfitted lavishly as regular visitors at Maison Worth, and at the atelier of Madame Vionnet, on L'Avenue Montaigne. How many hours Ophelia had stood, in one pose and then another, as satins, tulles, and velvets were draped and pinned, silks held to her face. Her mother had insisted on several suitably virginal evening gowns in white, embroidered in silver thread, as well as crêpe day dresses in pastel hues. There was new riding attire, head-dresses of ostrich feathers, and shoes dainty of heel, destined to be danced to their graves upon the polished floors of London residences.

Ophelia had embraced the novelty, having been previously confined to sensible wool for winter and summer cottons.

For Lady Finchingfield, as chaperone, the Season would be almost as onerous. In gold brocade and lamé, diamonds glittering, she had every intention of rising to the occasion. Her dark-haired beauty had been admired in her youth and was admired still.

Upon her return to London, Ophelia had completed a course of instruction under the Vacani sisters at their studio in South Kensington, learning the waltz, foxtrot and polka. In preparation for her presentation at Court, she was also schooled on the finer points of the deep curtsey she would perform, first to King George, and then to his consort, Queen Mary.

'Keep your back straight at all times,' commanded the first Miss Vacani.

'Bend at the knee, your eyes ever upon the King,' urged the second.

'Smile as you rise, and you may receive a returning smile of approval,' continued the first.

The two were always finishing each other's sentences. Ophelia thought of them as a pair of budgerigars, contentedly preening and casting a twinkling eye on those about them.

However, she couldn't help feeling that the experience was designed to subjugate her—to place her neatly in a box, from which she should seek to charm without uttering a single original thought. Speaking at all, it appeared, was to be undertaken with caution.

'Say as little as is needed. Absence of conversation is no impediment to success in gaining a man's interest,' her mother had advised on the evening before it all began. 'Moreover, never meet a man's gaze directly. They find it intimidating, as if we were probing their mind.'

Ophelia wondered what she might be expected to find there...

Lady Finchingfield's advice appeared unending.

'And it doesn't do to let others know of your cleverness, Ophelia. Men fear that a woman who is too clever—by which they mean the slightest cleverness at all—is not theirs to control. Better to put that cleverness to covert use. Once married, a woman can achieve much behind the scenes.'

Ophelia didn't see why her achievements, whatever they might be, shouldn't be celebrated in the same way as a man's. Nevertheless, she bowed to her mother's wisdom in matters relating to the "handling" of men. Her own father acceded to Lady Finchingfield in all matters of Society and the household, and seemed to consider himself fortunate in being able to do so.

To begin her debutante Season, at last, had been a relief. The lessons and lectures were over. Once Ophelia threw herself into the thing she'd be able to steer her own path, she felt sure.

She'd been ready to enjoy herself. After all, there would be hundreds of men; some of them would be charming and handsome, surely! And new girls to become chummy with. Endless possibilities!

Except that so many of the men turned out to be sly weasels or ebullient stags, and the girls seemed much younger than herself. Back at Girton, she'd sometimes found her fellow students rather too studious, but she yearned, now, for their sincere discussions—that had nothing to do with whether a certain shade of yellow made the wearer appear bilious.

Most mornings involved riding in Hyde Park, along Rotten Row and Ladies' Mile, returning to a formal breakfast of kippers, omelette, and grilled kidneys. Besides concerts, garden parties, and picnics, there were polo and cricket matches to watch and croquet and lawn tennis to play. Ophelia even tried her hand at archery and at bowls.

The social round was relentless. Ophelia's enthusiasm quickly waned for evenings spent among a hundred other guests crammed into a first-floor drawing room in Belgravia or Mayfair, converted into a ballroom for the night. At the opera no one listened, while at the ballet no one watched. It was all too apparent that the real purpose was to be seen.

Accustomed to falling into bed exhausted, usually no earlier than two in the morning, Ophelia had wondered how she'd maintain the pace. By the time her own debutante ball arrived, her feet would be worn to stumps. Regardless, she'd have no choice but to endure the clutches of every decrepit old wart and every young toad wishing to shuffle her about.

Ophelia's little Cairn, Pudding, was most affronted by her mistress' new social habits, since it left her scarce time to bestow the tickles the terrier's soft little belly expected.

Ophelia's mother appeared to enjoy the experience far more than Ophelia. She certainly drew more admirers. Other chaperones sat quietly dozing over their knitting. Lady Finchingfield, statuesque and resplendent in her Paris fashions, attracted not only an assortment of middle-aged fathers but several of the most eligible gentlemen.

In fact, there was little need for her mother to court favour on Ophelia's behalf, since the family's wealth alone inspired others to solicit her presence. Ophelia's father, Sir Peter Finchingfield, MP for King's Lyppe, was only distantly related to blue blood but he was heir to a successful turkey farming business. Meanwhile, as a rising star in the Conservative party, he was tipped for a cabinet position, having recently led a vital debate in the House on subsidisation of root vegetable growing, with particular reference to swedes and turnips.

What Sir Peter lacked in charm was provisioned by Lady Finchingfield, herself the daughter of a noble family, though one of constrained means. She believed in her own infallible taste—in clothes, literature, art, music, and interior décor. It was of no regard that her acquaintance with them resembled that of a bee flitting from flower to flower, without collecting a grain of pollen. In her eyes, all things connected with herself were highly sought after and, since social standing and money happily met in the Finchingfield household, the world at large was disposed to agree.

At least I'll wake up far away from her!

Ophelia punched the pillow before flopping back upon it.

Where had it all gone wrong?

She couldn't blame her mother entirely. From the first, it had been Ophelia herself who'd encouraged Percival; or, at least, she hadn't discouraged him.

Not that they'd spent an inordinate amount of time together, but it seemed courtships happened swiftly, whenever two were fortunate enough not to find each other unduly repulsive.

Ophelia had been wearing her mauve silk, she recalled, at their first meeting. Not her best colour, though the cornflowers embroidered from shoulder to hem were rather pretty.

She'd had a headache and had tried to plead off attending yet another soirée, but her mother had been a gorgon about it. Retreating to an alcove, Ophelia had though herself safe from the hubbub but a portly gentleman, seemingly with some standing as a manufacturer in the northern counties, had cornered her and begun describing, at some length, the procedure for making clothes pegs.

She'd been all too glad when Percival had presented himself to escort her to the buffet. Well-mannered and agreeable, though sporting the pimples of youth and an over-fondness for hair oil, Percival was perfectly pleasant, albeit with a limited repertoire in small talk.

It didn't take long to gather that interbreeding by certain old families had bestowed upon him a brain never intended for strenuous exercise, but Ophelia had smiled and held her tongue, assuming an expression of rapt fascination as Percival inventoried his last "bag" of hare, duck and goose, partridge and pheasant. By all accounts, it had been the most successful of shooting seasons.

They'd next met within the marbled and mirrored halls of Grosvenor House—this time, Ophelia wearing sequinned dancing shoes, fastened with diamanté buttons, and a shimmering silver gown. Percival had rescued her from a retired major whose toupée, in vivid tangerine, would have looked quite at home in the jungles of Borneo. Having swooped in, he took her hand and led her into the throng for a foxtrot, and she'd been more than willing to overlook a few crushed toes.

By their third meeting Ophelia, demure in rose-coloured silk, had begun to view him as a good egg. He'd partnered her at supper, eaten without spilling anything over her or himself, and had given her a chaste kiss upon the forehead on departure, uttered with a cheery 'toodle-pip'.

The following evening, they'd taken lemon ices on a balcony at the Connaught Hotel, where tulips, apple blossom, and rhododendrons spilled from vases and arum lilies and climbing roses swathed a glass wall, floodlit from behind. Ophelia, this time wearing buttercup yellow embellished with tiny violets at the neck and hem, had allowed Percival's aristocratic hand to creep about her waist. She'd prepared herself for a "lunge" and had been all too ready to engage him on equal ground, but he'd merely given her a playful pinch and licked, somewhat provocatively, the cherry from the top of her sorbet.

In truth, it was Percival's lack of sexual guile, his very inexperience, that had soothed Ophelia.

It had been on the fifth evening of Ophelia's acquaintance with Percival that he'd escorted her from pre-dinner drinks at the Ritz to Devonshire House. Her mother had intentionally removed herself to a cab directly behind, whispering a hurried reminder to Ophelia that she be intelligent enough to conceal her intelligence.

Ophelia wasn't averse to wedlock as a means to further her social position, to secure her financial future, and to access a lifestyle that would include regular trips to the Continent and attendance at soirées hosted by the elite of her class. She hoped that her life might amount to more than choosing clothes and menus and entertaining people who bored her silly but she viewed marriage as a contract and, in signing it, was determined to acquire the very best terms.

As Lady Finchingfield would say, 'You were born, and you will die. What you make of the middle is your own affair.'

Percival had indeed seized the opportunity to make known his ardour. He'd clamped his wet lips to hers, tongue probing at her upper molars and, despite her utmost readiness to surrender to the moment, to allow Percival to prove himself masterful, Ophelia had been struck by a sense of absurdity.

She knew that wives were obliged to put up with things they found distasteful, and a woman's passions were secondary to those of her husband—if they existed at all.

As a radiant example of the innocent feminine, she was supposed to cast down her eyes and resist the eagerness of her suitor but in truth, physical intimacy was a subject she'd examined most thoroughly and with regular indulgence—often while daydreaming in a long, hot bath.

Rather than being coy, she looked forward to sampling the dishes of a lovers' table and believed there were all sorts of lovely things you might do with a husband, if he was amiable enough to experiment and not treat you like a statue of the Virgin Mary.

As Percival had withdrawn his tongue, dabbing saliva from the edges of his mouth, he'd extracted from his pocket a ring.

An alarmed repugnance had welled within Ophelia, surprising her in its vehemence.

There was the noose, and if she'd failed to wriggle free, she'd have found herself being kissed by Percival Huntley-Withington for the rest of her miserable life.

Ophelia reached plaintively for a caramel, but the train gave a lurch, and the Milk Tray almost took a tumble.

I suppose I should take that as a sign.

With a sigh, Ophelia replaced the lid and shoved the box under her pillow. One hardly needed to worry about one's waistline, thanks to current fashions, but she was loath to greet her grandmother on the morrow with an angry blemish erupting on the end of her nose.

Lady Finchingfield had forbidden cake or biscuits to pass her daughter's lips for months, for fear of Ophelia ruining her complexion, and her chance of a desirable match alongside.

Not that any of that matters now!

Buried in the depths of the Highlands, husband-material was likely to be sparse. Anyone on the marriage-mart would be in London, where the Season still had a few weeks to go before everyone scampered off to the country again, or headed to the Continent for some late summer sun.

Scotland was going to be a wilderness on all fronts.

There was only one consolation, and that was a titbit scrawled at the bottom of her grandmother's last letter. With her birthday on the horizon, she was having a rather modish artist paint her portrait.

Despite her forebodings, Ophelia could not deny a certain excitement.

There was probably little else to do in Caledonia but sit about having yourself immortalized, and those grand castles of old had plenty of wall space for the canvases.

In fact, wild Bohemians are probably thicker on the ground in the Highlands than they are in Bloomsbury. They'll be everywhere, painting grand views and sighing for a muse.

Naturally, those sorts would be expertly experienced, being marvellous kissers and much besides.

Ophelia closed her eyes and wriggled under the covers. Hugging her faithful terrier, she drifted into delicious dreams.

As the miles passed under the wheels of the Scotch Express, Ophelia saw herself reclined upon a chaise longue, draped in nothing but a length of chiffon. Her imagination conjured for her a brooding,

Byronic artist, eyes seared with yearning. Overcome with desire, he covered the room in a great bound and tore the diaphanous wisp of fabric away, crushing her lips to his.

By the time the whistle blew to announce their crossing of the border, young Ophelia Finchingfield had been most thoroughly and satisfyingly ravished.

2

A RUDE INTRODUCTION

THE LAST HOUR OF THE TRAIN JOURNEY, FOLLOWING HER CHANGE ONTO a rackety branch line, took Ophelia truly into the depths of the towering Highlands, past fast-running streams and looming granite crags. Draped in mist, the violet sky overhung hillsides of russet and mustard.

When she emerged from her carriage, she found that the platform of her station comprised no more than some raised wooden boards placed at the side of the track. She looked about but there was no one to collect her, so Ophelia waited forlornly under a tree, water dripping down her collar. Pudding, being as averse to damp locks as her mistress, requested that she be held aloft, out of the puddles at Ophelia's feet.

It was a clear half hour before she heard the sound of a car engine.

The driver, rather than coming out to help her, honked the horn and motioned for Ophelia to climb in.

Bloody rude!

She wrenched open the door, breaking a nail in the process, and was obliged to bundle her own cases onto the back seat.

'Thank you ever so much,' she snapped, unpinning her sodden hat.

Pudding, nestled in her lap, eyed the stranger warily, her snout twitching.

'No trouble,' came the reply, in a Scottish accent, but clear enough for Ophelia to understand. 'I'm supposed to be felling trees today, but the rain made it difficult. Not so bad having to stop for a while to come and get you.'

The man behind the wheel was a rough-looking character in shabby clothing, unkempt, and with a beard full of hedgerow. He'd been undertaking manual labour, as was apparent not just from his appearance, spattered in woodchips and sawdust, but from the aroma filling the car—a cocktail of male sweat and damp tweed.

'Whisky?' he offered, passing a hip flask.

'Certainly not. It's eleven in the morning!'

'Please yourself.' He took a swig before stepping on the accelerator.

Horribly uncouth!

Ophelia fumed, her resentment growing.

And woefully undertrained.

'I say, please slow down.' The car took a bend at speed, jolting her sideways.

'I don't have all day London-Miss. Don't worry, I know these roads like the back of my hand.'

'I shall jolly well complain about you when we arrive. You're making me feel unwell with this awful handling of the car. You're not fit to drive!' argued Ophelia.

'Do as you like.'

She was too nauseated to argue.

The dense forest through which they motored soon opened out into a glen, hemmed in by steep-rising peaks, snow-topped despite the summer month. For some miles they passed only modest dwellings, few and far between. Turning towards the crags, they entered a tunnel through the rock and the car plunged into cool, silent darkness. They emerged upon the view of a great loch amid pinnacles black and barren.

At the water's edge stood the solid, grey stonework of a castle.

Beautiful yet mournful, the scene could have been one from an old Celtic tale. Nestled within its mountain embrace, Castle Kintochlochie looked ancient.

The car descended the hillside, sweeping to a halt before the stately home of generations of MacKintochs. Ophelia staggered out of the vehicle and managed three steps before ejecting the contents of her stomach.

She was watched with interest by the crowd gathered to welcome her—a party comprising her grandmother, Morag's companion Lady Devonly, and the entire staff of Castle Kintochlochie.

Pudding leapt from the car, joining Morag's Pekinese, and the two gave each other a cursory sniff before turning their attention to Ophelia's regurgitated porridge breakfast, hastily consumed on the train.

'Don't worry a bit,' said Lady Morag, stepping forward to take Ophelia's arm. 'The dogs'll clean it up in a jiffy. Let's get you inside.'

'Darling, you look so much like your mother,' Morag exclaimed, once Ophelia had joined her and Lady Devonly in the drawing room. The driver had absented himself but Ophelia made a mental note to relate her treatment at the first opportunity.

Tea poured and fruitcake eaten, Ophelia was feeling already rather better.

'What a sweet dog, my dear,' said Morag, giving Pudding a tickle beneath the chin. 'Such sympathetic company, aren't they? I wouldn't be without my darling Aphrodite.' The Pekinese, unwilling to endure another dog's monopoly of her mistress, abruptly barged the Cairn out of the way and offered herself in Pudding's stead.

Morag nodded to her companion. 'Perhaps you've heard of my dear friend Constance? A keen amateur naturalist and author of several acclaimed editions. We met while I was travelling in West Africa with my Angus, God rest his soul, making our study of the tribes of Dahomey.'

Looking about, Ophelia could see that the drawing room boasted ample evidence of those travels—a set of most alarming masks being placed upon the far wall, sporting what appeared to be real hair and teeth.

'You must look up Angus' book in the library, Ophelia dear. You are old enough, I think, to be exposed to its contents—*Courtship Customs of the Dahomey*. He published under a pseudonym, of course; there are limits to the tolerance of society, even as the new century progresses.

'Lady Devonly, married at the time to the British Ambassador, accompanied us on several trips into the interior, compiling her own fascinating catalogue of native parrot species. Take us as your example Ophelia; choose wisely, and marriage need not be too much of a bore.'

Constance smiled benignly and patted Ophelia's hand.

Morag continued, 'On this subject, I must agree with your mother that you've been rather naughty. An earldom is not to be sniffed at. Wedlock lends respectability.'

'I'm not a heifer to be purchased after inspection!' grumbled Ophelia.

Her grandmother held up one finger sternly, forbidding further interruption. 'Even though you'll come into your own fortune in a few years' time, you must consider your social position.'

Morag helped herself to a buttered muffin. 'Naturally, I can quite guess the truth of it. No doubt, you have a secret, vastly unsuitable lover.'

Ophelia decided to let Morag believe whatever appealed to her.

'Now, my dear, I'm all for a little harmless "sin" but a woman must, at last, select the right horse for her carriage. For a woman without choice, status, or education, marriage may be nothing but a contract for domestic and sexual services. As wives of a certain breeding and elevated class, we have the privilege to employ others to provide the first. As for the latter, wise is the wife who realizes that duties in the bedroom are of as much benefit to herself as to her husband.'

'Hmmm,' conceded Ophelia, her eyes a little misty.

Morag lowered her voice. 'My own marriage was a blissful joining of the sexes, founded on equality of intellect and passion. Not so my brother Ebenezer, whose bride ran away with the gamekeeper. He has never been the same. His own estate he gambled away and has spent most of his life in abject resentment.'

Morag's gaze wandered towards the window, seeming to see other times, other places. When she looked back, her eyes were perhaps a little more alive with those remembrances.

'My darling husband, having the empathy of the angels, insisted that Ebenezer should live out his days with us, but I fear the arrangement is not always inclined to make us merry. The state of his hinges has been long under debate.'

Ophelia, pouring everyone another cup of tea, wondered if she might help herself to a third slice of cake.

Pudding watched closely the movement of fingers from plate to mouth and back again. If a crumb were to drop, she wished to be ready.

Morag continued, 'Of course, there's Hamish, Constance's nephew. Darling boy has been with us about five years now, managing the estate. He's a wonderful help, so practical! Spends much of his time in the forest cabin. It's his way of coping. So much tragedy; a man needs to keep busy...'

Ophelia wondered what tragedy her grandmother was referring to, but thought it might be impolite to ask for further details.

'You'll meet Ebenezer this evening. Poor thing has been suffering with the flu. He's been creeping towards the grave so long that the Reaper has grown tired of waiting for him to shamble within arm's reach. My side of the family are known to live to at least ninety,' added Morag. 'Even then, they're usually sent into the hereafter by acts of over-exuberance rather than poor constitution. My own father was fit as a fiddle until the day he died, a week before his centenary. He was in the pigsty, giving his prize porker a rub down; the details are shadowy but he was found with the sow sitting comfortably on his chest.'

Ophelia, startled by this revelation, dropped the muffin she was about to bite into. It had hardly touched the rug before Pudding leapt forward to claim it, carrying off her prize to a defensible position

27

beneath the sideboard. Aphrodite, rounder of belly, and clearly less nimble, was left snuffling at the crumbs.

'You must tell us about Paris, dear,' Constance prompted. 'It's so long since I've been. Are the women still as chic? I recall their corsets being laced so tightly that they daren't even laugh. I could never wait until the end of the day to ease mine off. You're lucky to have avoided those fearsome contraptions. Today's fashions are much less constricting.'

'It was wonderful,' Ophelia began, relating some of her excursions and adventures. 'Even under the watchful eye of Mother, between clothes fittings and endless trips to galleries, I tasted a little of the Bohemian lifestyle—artists lounging in cafés, discussing all manner of topics.'

How many times had Ophelia strained to listen, employing her schoolgirl French to eavesdrop on those conversations. Breathing the Parisian air had surpassed all expectations. The place positively buzzed with possibilities.

'Ah yes,' sighed Constance, recalling her own youthful days in that enchanting city.

'We're generally quiet here, my dear,' Morag added. 'None of the glitz of the City of Light, but we have all sorts of fun planned for the coming days. It's not every week that a woman turns sixty. I'm determined to do so in style.'

The grandfather clock in the hallway began its long chimes.

'Ah, it's past midday.' Lady Morag beckoned the butler forward. 'Haddock, it's time for a cocktail. Three gin fizzes if you please.'

3

ARTISTIC GENIUS

'My angel, what a pretty dress!' said Morag, leading Ophelia into the dining room that evening. She pinched Ophelia's cheek fondly, admiring the green taffeta with geometric designs around the hem. 'And such jolly company we make.'

'Tripe!' proclaimed Ebenezer.

Ophelia was inclined to agree, looking at the fearsome visage of her great-uncle and the army of atrocious ancestors glaring at her from the walls—the eyes of some disdainful, others demented. They might look distinguished, but they hardly appeared likable.

'So difficult to find suitable guests,' Morag conceded. 'Just us I'm afraid, and our 'resident artist', Mr. Launcelot Buffington. Most of our neighbours are half-wits, and the rest have criminal tendencies. There's barely a teaspoon to be found after they've visited.'

Ophelia's first impression of Mr. Buffington was somewhat disappointing. His age was indeterminate, his chin was on the weak side, and he lacked the height she found naturally appealing in the male sex. However, his attire was suitably artistic. Besides the addition of an embroidered waistcoat, he wore a large, pink enamelled lily pinned to his jacket.

Morag indicated a newly hung canvas above the mantelpiece, cloaked in a swathe of velvet.

'I have a surprise for you all. Mr. Buffington has completed his portrait of me. We'd planned to unveil it at my grand party, but I simply cannot wait.'

Ophelia smiled at her grandmother's evident excitement. Meanwhile, Haddock began serving from a tureen of pea soup.

'I was reading a fascinating article in *The Lady*,' continued Morag. 'It was all about Mr. Buffington, talking about his marvellously modern approach. He has lately been in his botanical phase, by which he ascertains the personality of his subject and renders their psyche, in all its complexities, through the metaphor of edible root and leaf.'

'How...original!' commented Ophelia, not knowing quite what to say. She too had seen the piece, her mother being a subscriber to *The Lady*. She hoped Mr. Buffington's choice would be neither unflattering, nor too obvious in the rendering.

Had the Tate not taken up Mr. Buffington as a genius of his time, Ophelia wondered whether his clients might have objected to being likened to turnips and swedes, although, from her own experience, more than a handful bore strong resemblance to those most solid of British vegetables.

Mr. Buffington extracted a lace handkerchief from his upper pocket, with which he dabbed his eyes. 'Lady MacKintoch's invitation to paint her portrait could not have come at a more welcome time. I am lately besieged by those enamoured of my talents! Day and night, I have no peace, the cultured elite ever requesting the flourish of my brush. They are drawn like moths to the flame, only to have their wings scorched when they discover that my fire burns purely for my artistry. Paint and canvas are my lovers; to them alone can I be true.'

'I'm yet to discover what botanical he has ascribed to me,' added Morag. 'The artistic process is most mysterious. I do not presume to speculate. The higher, artistic mind will decide.'

At one end of the table, Ebenezer cleared his throat lustily, sending a gobbet of phlegm into his bowl. He stirred it round, then continued to administer soup to his lips.

'I can wait no longer,' asserted Morag, her voice quivering with excitement. 'Mr. Buffington, if you please...'

He rose from the table and, with a grand flourish, whipped off the drape.

'I say!' remarked Ophelia. Something else seemed required, so she ventured, 'Wonderful composition and use of colour.'

The canvas showed Morag reclined upon a chaise, with a basket of bananas covering her modesty. Her body was half human half pineapple, the leaves of which emerged Gorgon-like from her head. In either hand, she clutched a satsuma, placed strategically before each ample bosom.

'Extraordinary!' added Ophelia. 'So... fecund. Reminding us that we are, after all, creations of nature.'

'Brava, dear,' said Constance. 'I had faith that you'd inspire something out of the ordinary. And congratulations to our artist in residence.'

Mr. Buffington bowed deeply, a flush of pleasure suffusing his cheeks.

'Wonderfully exotic!' enthused her grandmother. 'But I must also express my thanks to dear Haddock, who sustained me through all those hours of sitting still. What would I have done without his steady supply of hot crumpet? It was awfully chilly posing in my nudey-nakedness.' She gave a titter.

Ebenezer snorted. 'Minions of Satan! You'll all roast in Hell.' He sucked the last of his soup noisily from his spoon.

Ophelia stifled a laugh. Morag and Constance seemed to be ignoring the outburst, but Mr. Buffington looked away uncomfortably.

Meanwhile, the butler and footman cleared the first course and brought in the next, all the while discreetly avoiding eye contact with the portrait or anyone about the table.

'Ah!' Morag announced. 'Saddle of venison, served with potatoes Lyonnaise and baby artichokes. Not a day goes by that I don't give thanks for our cook, Mrs. Beesby. She's such a wonder!'

Ophelia, feeling decidedly peckish, was glad to note an absence of cabbage. She helped herself to a dollop of currant sauce, held at her shoulder by the footman.

The food was, indeed, delicious, such that the party fell to silence for a few moments in their enjoyment and, in truth, being at a loss as how best to comment further upon the revelation above the mantelpiece.

At last, Constance broke the spell of contemplative mastication. 'How is your Season going, my dear? Have you made new friends?'

Ophelia answered readily. 'I did meet two lovely sisters, Baba and Nancy Beaton, whose brother, Cecil, takes the most delightful photographs. He's promised to take mine one day.'

'Divine!' pronounced Mr. Buffington. 'Cecil has the most marvellous sensibilities.'

'And what of the Bright Young Things, dear? Are you one of their merry band?' enquired Constance.

Ophelia grimaced. 'My mother vetoed any invitation that appeared unsuitable. I heard about midnight car chases and other escapades, of course. I'd have loved to attend Elizabeth Ponsonby's 'bath and bottle' party.

Haddock placed a dish of raspberry mousse before her, into which Ophelia plunged her spoon.

'They had the most spiffing time at St. George's Swimming Baths. I heard the dowagers sat like plump hens roosting, watching all the 'improper' behaviour through their lorgnettes.'

'What fun!' interjected Morag. 'I've been missing out!'

Ophelia continued excitedly. 'There was a top-notch band from New York, playing the latest jazz. They danced until dawn and then spilled out to catch buses, still wearing their bathing costumes. Can you imagine! The newspapers called it depraved.'

A low grumble emerged from Ebenezer, whose eyebrows were knotting fiercely with each revelation.

'Baba tells me there was a lot more going on in the pool besides swimming,' Ophelia added with relish.

'Nancy boys and mental defectives!' barked Ebenezer, his moustache twitching.

'I'm all for young people's frivolity. We who sent our men to fight in that dreadful war can be so dour.' Morag's gaze fell upon the family crest on her dessertspoon.

'My dear Angus and my son—your uncle Teddy, Ophelia—both fell at the Somme.' She raised her eyes and gave a small smile. 'Let the young have their fun. Let them live. There's been enough darkness.'

Kintochlochie's cattle, the fish in its rivers and lochs, and the trees upon its sprawling estate are maintained by a great many who go mostly unseen. The same is largely true of those who dust, and polish, and lay fires in the house, who launder clothes, and shine shoes, who make beds and serve, from before first morning light until the last hot-water bottles and cups of cocoa.

If you were to travel down the backstairs of the castle, and along a corridor that saw never enough natural light and was far from the warmth of any fire, you'd arrive in the kitchens. There, if you cared to linger, you'd overhear views different from those in the upper dining hall.

The servants of Kintochlochie, like those in every grand residence, have their own opinions on goings-on. They observe what others do not.

As on many other nights, the young footman, McFinn has sat down to his mutton stew, while Mr. Haddock continues serving digestifs in the drawing room. Mrs. Beesby has poured herself a small sherry and settled herself in front of the hearth. Una, the scullery maid, was elbow deep in suds and tableware...

'Don't be scratching the embossed gold, Una,' warned the cook. 'We're taking off the grease, nae the pattern.'

'I swear no one needs this much glassware for one dinner!' grumbled Jennet, whose task was to dry and polish.

'I heard that.' Mrs. Beesby frowned. 'Just you wait. We'll soon be having guests upon guests arriving. You'll have summat to moan about then!'

'Nice dumplings, Mrs. B,' interjected McFinn, giving a wink and holding one up for admiration on the end of his fork.

'Haud yer wheesht,' smiled the cook. 'We're too tired for that malarkey!'

'Some nice'uns upstairs too, courtesy of our London miss. Like her mother I recall, when she was here in 1921. Just started I was, doin' all the dirty jobs.' He chewed contemplatively. 'Lady Finchingfield's charms were always well on display, no matter how cold it were.'

'Less o' that from you, McFinn,' admonished Mrs. Beesby, 'or I'll have Mr. Haddock dock your wages!'

'Just saying,' answered McFinn, grinning through a mouthful of suet pudding.

4

SEDUCTION INTERRUPTED

IT WAS AT BREAKFAST THE FOLLOWING DAY THAT MORAG PLACED HER hand upon Ophelia's and informed her that nothing would give her greater pleasure than to see Mr. Buffington complete a portrait of her granddaughter.

'You look so much as I did, Ophelia, as a young woman. How lovely it would be to have your painting hang in my bedroom. There is something not just in your features but in your eyes I recognise. It would do me good to have that twinkle appraise me each morning when I wake.'

It was not an offer Ophelia could refuse and, in truth, the idea appealed to her vanity. To be immortalised on canvas is to live forever. Photography, wonderful as it was, simply did not compare. How she would love to be the subject of a portrait, to participate in its creation, rather than simply analyse it as she had done during her Girton studies.

Although it was only her second day at Castle Kintochlochie, it seemed that her wanton imaginings might be conjured into reality. Mr. Buffington was no Byron, but nor was he a spotty adolescent or a desiccated lecher. His conversation was more flamboyant than she considered desirable, but he was certainly not dull; the waters irrigating his brain were far from brackish.

Coddled egg eaten and coffee drunk, Mr. Buffington appeared to escort her across the garden to the summerhouse he had equipped as a studio.

'How wondrous is the air! The crags! The very grass we walk upon! An artist cannot thrive in the city. Creativity is born of natural beauty,' exclaimed Mr. Buffington. 'Behold this majestic cow.' He gestured towards a nearby shaggy specimen, its ginger fringe flopping into its eyes as it chewed a particularly luscious mouthful of Kintochlochie grass. 'Such a regal beast! Who knows what grand philosophies it may ponder.'

'They do have a certain charm,' mused Ophelia.

Pudding, trotting beside them, also scrutinised the beast and made mental note of her own superiority. Despite her legs being certainly shorter, Pudding could move at lightning speed when adequately moti-vated. The merest sniff of a custard cream was enough to ignite the flame, and her propulsion appeared to occur without legs at all, her undercarriage being thick with fluff.

'They are the aristocracy of the field.' Launcelot's hand fell upon his heart. 'Such beasts connect us to the long arm of history as much as the cool stones of Castle Kintochlochie and its glorious inhabitants of old. What stories this cow might tell were it to gain the power of speech.'

'I think this particular cow isn't more than a few months old,' Ophelia pointed out. 'But perhaps animals can converse with one another,' she added, wishing to be kind. 'Who's to say they don't pass down their bovine secrets.'

They both looked at the calf, which looked back at them, its gums smacking in contemplative reverie.

To Ophelia's astonishment, Mr. Buffington took her face between his cool palms, his eyes alight with emotion.

'I see that you too possess a soul in tune with nature's grandeur. You are, no doubt, in sympathy with all that is most beautiful, from the ancient and modern world.'

He dropped a kiss upon her fingers. 'Now, my dear, let's get your clothes off and get some paint slapped on a canvas!'

~

Ophelia desired to flirt and be flirted with. While Launcelot Buffington was not a man with whom she wished to spend the rest of her life, she'd "give him a go", and sample whatever erotic thrills he might provide. She allowed the golden brocade supplied for her pose to slip more than a little from her shoulder.

'I hope I'm not moving about too much for you,' enquired Ophelia, angling herself forward on the divan, to present her cleavage to best advantage.

Pudding swivelled her eyes upward with some resentment. Her place was not upon the floor but next to Ophelia, wherever she might sit or lie.

'Hmm. Try to keep still if you can,' Launcelot replied, applying a touch of vermillion to his mixing palette. He found skin tone such a challenge; Ophelia's left nipple was proving a particular trial.

'You have a spiritual temperament, sensitive to nature's vibrations, Mr. Buffington.' Ophelia dropped her eyes demurely, while tweaking the fabric to reveal a good deal more above the knee.

'Quite so.' Mr. Buffington daubed more paint. 'And do call me Launcelot. We're all friends here.'

'Absolutely. And I feel convinced that you are also a man of physical passion, as all men should be.'

'I leave others to judge,' answered Launcelot, sucking pensively on the end of his brush. 'All things in moderation…'

Ophelia was just pondering how far she could shift the drape without it falling altogether when a great furry hound lolloped through the door.

Braveheart, who had been busy on a bone-burying mission, was ready to take his usual place out of the wind upon the floor of the summerhouse, which was warm with sunshine at this time of day. A wolfhound's needs are modest, as those of most dogs are.

Braveheart was somewhat surprised to find his regular lazing spot inhabited by others, but not deterred. His loping stride brought him first to Mr. Buffington, who gave him a friendly pat upon the head, and then to the newcomer of the party, for an affable sniff. He was delighted to find Ophelia a first-class scratcher of ears. He had just given her toes a grateful lick when he became aware of hot breath upon his fur, somewhere about the shin.

A low, throaty rumble came from the floor, a guttural gargle reminiscent of bronchial congestion.

Braveheart's eyes were not what they once were, and he was blissfully unaware of the coming danger.

'Now then!' warned Ophelia. 'Make friends!'

The matter, in Pudding's mind, had already been settled. She'd been in residence for at least a full day, and the summerhouse (along with the rest of the castle and its grounds) was now hers. She ruled wherever her dainty paws passed, and they had claimed possession.

Precisely three dog heartbeats later, Pudding's growl became a piercing battle cry and, to Braveheart's dismay, the terrier's tenacious teeth clamped upon his lean leg.

The wolfhound gave a yelp.

'Naughty Pudding!' admonished Ophelia, bending to intervene.

A tall figure had followed Braveheart into the summerhouse, appearing at the doors just at the moment of hostility.

'What the hell!' the voice declared, and much besides.

Ophelia delivered a sharp poke under Pudding's armpit, which worked a treat in persuading the dog to relinquish her grasp.

Clasping the struggling bundle to her chest, Ophelia sat up. She recalled the thick Scottish lilt of the voice and the face was one she recognised. His nose looked to have been broken at some point and he had a scar above his right eyebrow. It was a powerful face; heavily freckled, battered by the sun and wind. The intruder was none other than her ruffian driver, his eyes wild and a vein throbbing in his temple.

Ophelia endeavoured to regain her composure. 'Pudding never usually behaves badly. She was caught by surprise. Whoever owns this dog needs to keep a firmer hand.'

The ruffian's mouth was set in an angry line, his tone furious. 'It's my dog, and I'll bid you to keep yours under control!'

The wolfhound had lost no time in removing himself and, wracked with self-pity, was licking his ill-used shin.

Ophelia cradled the squirming terrier in her arms and held her tight, giving her an abrupt tap on the nose. What she whispered in the dog's ear was between Pudding and her mistress.

The man was on his knees now, assessing Braveheart's injury. Fortunately, Pudding's savagery had been more in thought than in deed, and the skin was unbroken.

'Bloody irresponsible, letting your dog attack like that,' snapped the Scot, although with less venom than before.

'No harm done!' interjected Mr. Buffington, from behind the safety of his easel. 'Set the dogs a good example now. No need for us to bare our teeth.'

The intruder stood. 'I'll leave you to it…whatever "it" is.' His tone was scathing. 'Come on, Braveheart, nothing here for us.'

Ophelia lowered her eyes, all too aware of how much of herself was on show.

~

'I wonder if these were the ones she wore to be presented at Court, with all those other debutantes,' pondered Maggie, holding up a pair of Ophelia's silk knickers (dove grey and trimmed with French lace, at twelve shillings a pair). 'She might've had these under her finery, to see the King and Queen, all jangling in their priceless jewels.'

'The elastic's a bit loose. Lucky they didn't fall down as she made her courtesy,' said Nessa. 'Will she notice if they "go missing" do ye think?'

'Best leave alone,' advised Maggie. 'They look new enough.'

'They say even the Queen's nightgown has diamonds on it. Bit uncomfortable if you ask me,' said Nessa, pouring hot water in the laundry tub.

'Dinna ken why it's us lumbered with the extra laundry. You'd think Mary had enough time on her hands. Miss Hoity Toity, upstairs all the day long, seeing to her ladyship and Lady Devonly,' grumbled

Maggie. 'Not as if they change costume more than two or three times a day. She's more leisure than the rest of us put together.'

'Snooty cow,' agreed Nessa, shaking in the soap. 'Trays in her room all the time; too good to sit wi' the likes of us!'

'I'm right narked!' said Maggie. 'Thinking I might be better off working in a teashop or some such. I've a fancy to go to Inverness. I've an aunt on Chapel Street would have me. Short days, decent pay and tips!'

She looked ruefully at a gusset. 'Got to be better than this!'

'Perhaps I'll come with you,' said Nessa, giving Maggie a nudge. 'Your aunt got room for two?'

'Leave off. We cannae both bolt. Someone needs to see to their whims.'

'I wouldnae go anyway,' sniffed Nessa. 'I've the biggest of the servant's rooms after Cook and Mr. Haddock, with the old rug from Lady Devonly's room on the floor, and my own sink. Right nice it is. No one else is having it.'

'Easily pleased you are,' retorted Maggie. 'Watch out or you'll live and die in service. Sink or no sink!'

5

AN ANNOYING ATTRACTION

OPHELIA SAT UPON THE EDGE OF HER BED, EATING A BAR OF FRY'S Chocolate she'd had buried in the pocket of her coat.

Morag's maid, Mary, had laid out several evening dresses for her to choose from, left behind by Ophelia's mother a few years ago on one of her rare visits.

None were in the latest fashion, and they were far more Lady Finchingfield's style than her own, but Ophelia was short of options. There hadn't yet been time to press all the clothes she'd brought up on the train.

What Ophelia did notice was that the dresses were far more daring than the clothes Lady Finchingfield had purchased for her daughter to wear.

She picked up one of the gowns in dark blue silk and let it slither over her head. It reached fully to the floor, was high-necked at the front, and plunging at the back. She vaguely remembered her mother wearing it for a special party and having her photo taken for the Society pages. It was hardly the thing for a draughty Scottish castle. However, the colour was becoming, and the fabric was divinely soft against her skin.

Perhaps if I wear the drop garnet earrings from my birthday, and try a dark lipstick.

It felt deliciously naughty to wear something of her mother's. Lady Finchingfield had always been strict about Ophelia not borrowing from her wardrobe.

That settles it, thought Ophelia. *I'm wearing you! And let's see what we can get up to together.*

~

By the time Ophelia entered the drawing room for pre-dinner cocktails, the others had assembled. Morag and Constance were on their second glass of sherry, Launcelot had mixed himself a martini, and the whisky decanter was seeing considerable action in the vicinity of Ebenezer's tumbler.

'Ah, here's Ophelia!' announced Morag, sweeping forward to embrace her. 'Darling, how elegant you look; all grown up.'

She ushered forward a woman, who was all smiles and tight grey curls.

'I want you to meet an old friend of mine, Ophelia. The last time she saw you, I believe you were about three years old, so I don't suppose you remember her. This is Ms. Ellingmore.'

'What a pleasure,' answered Ophelia. 'My friends and I love your novels.'

'Just what all authors love to hear. Thank you, my dear.' Ms. Ellingmore beamed. 'And do call me Enid.'

'What Enid doesn't know about the antics of the aristocracy isn't worth knowing, from a novelist's point of view,' commented Constance, coming over to join them.

'Just remember that everyone of Enid's acquaintance is in danger of appearing within her pages,' teased Morag. 'The leading lady of *On Soaring Wings* owes more than a little to my younger self.'

In truth, Ophelia had read only two of Ms. Ellingmore's titles — *Unchained Love* and *Hearts Rampant*—but recalled that the storylines bore little resemblance to reality. She supposed this was their attraction.

Ms. Ellingmore's heroines were disposed to extreme virtue, until the very moment of their willing seduction, and her villains were of the most dastardly hue. However, the two met in happy coincidence.

Sadly, the virginal maidens were invariably "saved" by a hero of vast moral superiority (though not until the reader had been permitted to devour several chapters of delicious error). Ophelia couldn't help but think that the heroines would have far more fun with the villains than with the heroes.

'Enid's current work is entitled *The Unfettered Damsel*,' explained Morag. 'She's setting it in a Scottish castle, so has come to soak up the atmosphere.'

'Novels!' barked Ebenezer. 'Sentimental rubbish and sensationalism!'

'No one is making you read them, Ebenezer!' retorted Morag. 'And do remember your manners. Enid's travelled a long way to visit us. She doesn't want to hear your rudeness.'

Enid, with admirable tolerance, waved away the offence and took Morag's arm. 'I'm of the conviction that fiction is filled with truths the heart dare not speak. It's there that young women, and men too if they've a mind, can explore the "what ifs" of life. It's in fiction that the heart dares to soar and the mind to leap beyond its confines.'

'Jolly good, Enid dear,' answered Morag. 'Constance and I have been reading your wonderful stories these last twenty years. They're just the ticket during the long winters up here.'

'Art, in all its forms, provides nourishment for the soul,' agreed Launcelot. 'The arts are my spiritual crusade, through which all envy and petty hatreds may be put aside.'

He popped the olive from his martini into his mouth and sucked it, with an expression of great thought.

'Hmmm,' said Ophelia. Her acquaintance with actors, writers, and artists was limited to those favoured by Lady Finchingfield, who liked to host cultural soirées. However, within their ranks, she'd observed violent jealousies of the most trivial kind. Launcelot's view of the world might be called overly-optimistic.

At that moment the door opened, and the wolfhound from the summerhouse entered, trotting straight to the fire to curl into a comfortable position.

Goodness me! thought Ophelia. *That dog gets everywhere.*

She'd left Pudding slumbering on her bed, which was probably just as well.

Close on the heels of the dog was its owner, the uncouth individual from earlier in the day—except that he appeared to have taken a bath and was significantly more groomed. Standing tall, the broadness of his chest was all too apparent, straining against the formality of his dinner jacket. Below the waist he was wearing a kilt of oranges and browns with a hint of green.

Ophelia let her gaze drop to the strangely enticing bit of leg showing above his dark socks.

Morag made the introduction. 'You've met, of course, dear. Our chauffeur, Brodie, is laid up with lumbago, otherwise he'd have met you from the station. I fear we shall have to retire him altogether. Hamish kindly stepped in, despite being so busy. He went straight up to the cabin afterwards, missing your first dinner with us. What would we do without you, Hamish?' added Morag, turning a smile of affection on him.

'The pleasure is always mine, Lady MacKintoch.' He gave her a small bow.

Ophelia had to concede that, now he was no longer filthy, there was something attractive about him. His auburn hair, now somewhat tamed, put her in mind of the wild Highlanders of yore.

Hamish, eyes a-glitter, looked at her with ill-concealed amusement and greeted her with a wry smile. 'Our delightful London guest, here to teach us true refinement.'

She glared. 'I'm sure that the ladies of this house have refinement in abundance.' Vowing that she'd be damned if she'd give him the satisfaction of seeing her squirm, she turned away.

At least she was wearing the silk dress. It made her a trifle chilled, but it allowed her the opportunity to show off the allure of her naked back.

They went into dinner and Ophelia found herself sitting somewhat distant from her nemesis. However, it took much self-control for her to avoid looking down the table at the infuriating Hamish. To her dismay, and excitement, it was apparent that he was not only attractive but a wit—being engaged in lively debate with Enid, Launcelot, and Morag. He seemed to have no trouble conjuring charming conversation for them.

Meanwhile, Ophelia was stuck beside Ebenezer and the demure Lady Devonly.

She ate largely in silence, growing ever more irritated. However, the meal itself was very good, and she felt compelled to offer her praise to her hostess.

Clearing her throat, Ophelia called down. 'The smoked trout pâté was divine, and the salmon en croute quite the best I've eaten anywhere.'

'All from the estate; I caught the trout and salmon myself this morning,' Hamish answered smartly.

'We're fortunate in our cook, Mrs. Beesby,' added Morag, 'but we must thank darling Hamish for providing us with the means for our supper tonight.'

'Perhaps he might take me out and show me how to catch them too,' Ophelia found herself saying, then cursing herself.

Fiddlesticks! He'll know I'm in a spin for him and his head is undoubtedly big enough as it is.

'Groping for trout!' interjected Ebenezer. 'A filthy euphemism! Keep a lookout Morag or they'll be rutting in the open air with the livestock!'

'Really Ebenezer! Not all young people are debauched, despite the jazz and flappers and what-not. Behave yourself!' commanded Lady MacKintoch.

Ophelia dared not look at Hamish, feeling that he would certainly be laughing at her now. Rutting indeed!

After dinner, as they gathered at the fire, Morag asked if Enid might recite some poetry. 'Something clever... some Edith Sitwell?'

'Drivelling idiotism,' grumbled Ebenezer.

Ms. Ellingmore began with an emotional air; clearly, Miss Sitwell was a favourite.

'What's the trollop saying?' grunted Ebenezer. 'Speak up. All this mumbling!'

'Ebenezer, you are too dreadful! What will our guests think?' Morag caught Ophelia's eye. 'Perhaps you might play us something on the piano, dear.'

Ophelia began with some pastoral pieces.

Ebenezer could be heard muttering, 'That instrument needs tuning again. Bloody awful racket!'

On a whim, she broke into the Gershwins' *Someone to Watch Over Me.* This delighted everyone; even Ebenezer stopped grumbling and began tapping his foot. She then played a chirpy rendition of *S'Wonderful.*

Ophelia had continued to avoid Hamish's eye but now found him at her elbow, the warmth of his body beside her on the piano stool. His thigh was undeniably pressed against hers. Despite his bath, a heady masculine aroma wafted from him. Caught between feelings of pleasure and embarrassment, she fought to control her blushes.

Her fingers stumbled over the keys, losing the thread of the tune completely.

'Don't worry, I've got this.' Hamish expertly took up the song. There was no denying that he could play. In fact, as he moved into an energetic rendition of *Sweet Georgia Brown*, it became clear that his mastery of the piano far surpassed Ophelia's own.

'Can't beat some decent jazz. We just need Louis Armstrong on his trumpet.' Hamish's eyes were alight with the music.

'I've most of the Creole Jazz Band's records,' said Ophelia. 'My mother hates all this, even though the BBC has been playing it on the radio. She says that it encourages riotous behaviour, but Daddy bought a gramophone and keeps bringing home new records. He's a fan too.'

'Do you remember, Constance,' mused Morag, 'When we stayed

with the Batammariba tribe for the Eho festival? The drumming went straight through your bones. We kicked off our shoes and joined in barefoot. This song makes me want to get up and do a jig.'

When Hamish finished with a flourish and began to pick out the melody of *Lady Be Good,* Ophelia ventured to join in again.

'Delightful, my darlings,' cooed Morag, 'The Gershwins are such a wonderful team, just as husband and wife should be—lyrics and music in perfect complement.'

'Bloody good I say. Makes a man feel half his age,' declared Ebenezer, looking remarkably perky.

'Hamish, it's been so long since I've heard you play. What a tonic!' beamed Constance. 'We must have this jolly music more often.'

Morag agreed. 'You've inspired us. Now, we ladies should repair to bed. Hamish, you'll stay up and play dominoes with Ebenezer, won't you. Haddock, some cocoa to my room as usual, please.'

As Ophelia retired, she saw Hamish tug his forelock and smirk in her direction.

She scurried to bed.

6

FOLLOWING ONE'S NATURAL INCLINATION

OPHELIA, COMING DOWN EARLY TO BREAKFAST, FOUND THE ONLY ONE at the table to be Hamish. She'd rather hoped it might be so. She'd chosen one of her most fetching tea dresses, in palest apple green cotton, and had tied a matching scarf round her head knotted just below her ear.

She helped herself from the hot buffet dishes and sat opposite, giving him an engaging smile.

'What are you up to today? More nude exhibiting?' he enquired, spreading raspberry jam thickly on a slice of toast. 'If you don't want an audience, perhaps consider closing the doors today so it's just you and the eminent Mr. Buffington. Although I have a feeling you may be sniffing in the wrong direction there.'

He gave her a grin and took a hefty bite.

The mackerel before her was blameless but Ophelia found herself looking at it most bitterly. She glowered at Hamish over the coffee pot, wishing that she could turn it into hemlock and pour him a cup.

Men! They're all the same. Too caught up in their own cleverness. Well, he won't be getting clever with me.

'Don't fret,' said Hamish, reading her expression. 'You won't have to look at my face too often. I usually grab breakfast in the kitchen and I'm not one for all this dressing for dinner. I often eat below stairs. I'm making special efforts to be sociable this week, it being Morag's birthday.'

'Too gracious of you, I'm sure!'

He stood to leave and, again, she was taken aback by the imposing physical presence of him. There was something about the very roughness of his manner that thrilled her, despite his rudeness.

She had a sudden vision of his hands, callused with their fingernails torn, reaching to lift her into his arms and his mouth, large and sensuous, closing upon hers.

'Most days, I stay up in the forest. There's a lot of clearing to be done. I sleep in the hillside cabin as much as I can; quieter there.'

'I'm sure it suits everyone that way,' Ophelia replied. 'Best not to inflict yourself on other people when you can't be civil.'

Mr. Buffington appeared then at the door and looked delighted to find Hamish and Ophelia alone.

'My darlings, the weather is remarkably fine. I propose a walk, Ophelia, before we knuckle down to the serious business of creating our art. We should begin by taking you around the loch. There's a breeze but in the sunshine nothing is better.'

'What a lovely invitation,' beamed Ophelia. 'I believe that Hamish is too busy to join us, however. He has some trees to cut down.'

She gave a haughty sidelong glare, then aimed her most radiant smile at Launcelot.

'Ah well, perhaps another time,' said Launcelot. 'Me and thee, young maiden, in half an hour? Perhaps we might conclude in the vegetable garden, in search of inspiration for your portrait.'

Launcelot and Ophelia promenaded companionably around the grand loch. As the rolling clouds parted golden beams darted across the purpled hillside while the water shimmered with white shards.

Surprised by the dancing of shade and light, deer, invisible to Ophelia until they lifted their heads, leapt away over splintered crags.

Pudding trotted contentedly at her mistress' side, her nose twitching at all the wonderful scents before her.

'How beautiful it is,' remarked Ophelia. 'Everything is so alive. It's as if I can hear the earth breathing, and the trees, although perhaps it's just a trick of the wind.'

Launcelot clasped her hands. 'You too have an artistic soul. You feel the fiercely living presence of this landscape.'

She smiled, realizing that although he was fascinatingly Bohemian, her insides simply weren't responding.

'You and I shall be friends Ophelia,' announced Launcelot. 'Whatever I can do to help you find your happiness in this world, you must tell me. I shall do my best to wave my brush, like a magical Godmother in a fairy-tale, to bring to life your secret wishes.'

'That may be the nicest thing that anyone has said to me.' Ophelia gave him a kiss upon the cheek. 'Thank you.'

After some time, they reached the castle's walled garden, where all manner of edibles were grown.

'An artist must respect even the smallest of God's creatures. This humble slug we might say is perhaps closer to Heaven than we poor sinners.' Mr. Buffington indicated a particularly fine, plump specimen, ingesting a cabbage leaf. 'It knows not greed, nor envy. On the day of reckoning, how many of its kind will rise to take their place with their maker? Why should not this simple slitherer know His grace?' Launcelot paused, adding dramatic piquancy to the image.

'Quite!' said Ophelia, feeling that some word of approbation was expected of her.

'Even this simple gastropod has the power to follow its heart's desire,' Launcelot mused.

The slug, in its noble mission, had been making good headway on the greens. Launcelot plucked it reverentially from the leaf upon which it feasted and held it aloft.

'Would that all men might follow their nature in the same fashion.'

'Absolutely,' agreed Ophelia. 'No point choosing a path against which your natural inclination rebels.'

'An artist must be free to express themselves, in all things. Liberation is essential.'

It was as they were walking towards the studio, and Launcelot paused to breathe the fragrance of a wild briar rose, that Ophelia saw his eyes swivel beyond her.

'And here approaches a form I would dearly love to capture on canvas,' he sighed.

A moment later from behind, and greatly to Ophelia's surprise, two sizeable hairy paws appeared upon her shoulders.

'Down, Braveheart!' came a familiar voice.

Pudding let out a series of yaps, causing Ophelia to fear the commencement of three rounds in the ring. However, upon hearing the tone of Pudding's command, Braveheart lay down at her feet and rolled over, presenting his belly in utter submission. Pudding accepted the gesture and pounced onto her supplicant's chest, giving the wolfhound's nose a lick.

'Well I never!' exclaimed Hamish. 'That's a first.'

'Ah yes!' replied Launcelot, looking up at Hamish through a flutter of lashes. 'In this place, I believe, everyone should succumb to Cupid's will.'

'Ha! There's a thought. Well, I won't argue. Not enough love in the world, I expect. Good job these two are getting on better anyway,' replied Hamish.

Pudding was now lying upon Braveheart's stomach, looking up at them from her comfortable cushion.

Hmmm, thought Ophelia. *He really can be rather pleasant when he puts his mind to it.*

'Sorry about that,' said Hamish, indicating the muddy paw prints on the shoulders of Ophelia's dress. 'Leave it to dry and it should brush off.'

'Now, my dear. Shall we return to that fetching pose?' interjected Launcelot. 'We can manage a good hour before the luncheon gong sounds. The studio should be delightfully warm with the sunshine beaming through the glass.'

As Ophelia resumed her position on the chaise longue, she found her thoughts wandering to the memory of Hamish's muscular thighs, the fabric of his trousers drawn taut by the wind.

'Dear one,' commented Launcelot cheekily, 'I do wonder, what *can* you be thinking of to cause such a dreamy expression?'

7

A TORMENTED PAST

IT WAS THE FOLLOWING DAY, LURED BY WONDERFUL SMELLS OF baking, that Ophelia found herself in the kitchen eating muffins hot from the oven topped with Mrs. Beesby's home-churned butter. The cook didn't stand on ceremony and soon put a bowl of egg whites into Ophelia's arms. Meringues didn't beat themselves.

'Sit doon, lassie, and we'll have a chitter-chatter,' said the cook.

It wasn't long before Mrs. Beesby was gossiping companionably. Despite herself, Ophelia couldn't resist turning the conversation to Hamish.

'Dearie me, so very sad. No man should have to suffer such torment—ah, the perils of childbirth. It's the Lord's way and we kinna argue,' lamented Mrs. Beesby. 'Nigh on five year ago he lost his wife, and his wee bairn. 'Twas a night as black as the Earl of Hell's waistcoat, and the mist thick all aboot the place, so the doctor couldnae reach the castle. Mr. Munro had only arrived a month, bein' in Edinburgh wi' his wife's folk afore that. Oh the tragedy!'

'How devastating…' choked Ophelia.

No wonder he so often retreated into the forest and spent much of his time alone.

I'm nothing but a beastly snob to make so many assumptions about the poor man.

~

Over the coming days, Ophelia had plenty of time to herself. Launcelot completed his painting of her—a not unpleasing rendition, in which her naked bottom took the form of a nectarine, and a runner bean ran the length of her spine. Morag was delighted and asked him to stay on to complete a landscape of the castle and its glen. There were plenty of vantage points from which to capture the view.

Hamish was notably absent, apparently spending much of his time on the wider estate and clearly content, Ophelia supposed, to enjoy the tranquillity of the forest cabin.

Morag, Enid, and Constance were always happy to include Ophelia in their conversation, but they tended to reminisce about times and places that meant little to her.

Dropping in on Mrs. Beesby, Ophelia began to feel that she might be under the cook's feet. She had a great many dishes to prepare for various dinners and the grand party planned.

Feeling restless, Ophelia took to roaming the castle's lesser-used wings and draughty corridors, musing on the forty-three generations who had done so before her. The dungeons, she'd heard, dated from the twelfth century.

It seemed that living in a state of permanent chill was the surest recipe for a long life, since innumerable aged Scots scrutinised her from their portraits. She imagined them rendered irritable by the scratchiness of their tartans and their icy beds.

Some parts of the castle were Spartan in appearance, cold seeping from the very stonework, and dust-faded furnishings. However, most of the living areas had been decorated luxuriously, warmed by dark oak panelling and tapestries. Frolicking satyrs appeared to be a favourite theme. There were heavy brocades at the windows, deep sofas, and plump cushions.

Her room was no exception, boasting purple velvet drapes, and a small bookcase of French novels, Russian poetry, and the plays of Oscar Wilde. Directly before the fire, an inviting wing-backed chair became Ophelia's favourite nook to sit and read.

Her bedchamber could not have been more in contrast with her lace-frilled room in London. Decorated in shades of peach, it was her mother's idea of a fitting place for a young virgin to sleep.

However, she'd soon exhausted her own bookcase and, deciding that her mind was in need of improvement, resolved upon scouring the library for its most serious titles. In truth, there seemed to be a wealth of these kinds of editions, their pristine covers indicating that few had ever been opened.

Tucking herself into an old leather armchair, with Pudding alongside, Ophelia had just begun flipping through *Livestock Husbandry for the Highlands* when she heard Hamish calling for Braveheart.

The next moment, Hamish was approaching the fire. Turning, he saw her and started in surprise.

Ophelia closed the volume promptly.

'What *are* you reading?' Hamish peered at the edition in her lap. 'I can lend you something cheerier if you're bored. Or wouldn't you prefer one of Enid's books?'

Ophelia rolled her eyes. 'Just because I like novels doesn't mean I can't read serious books too. I thought this might be rather useful. The illustrations are very odd though.'

'Probably because it's an antique,' said Hamish, obviously amused. 'Look in the flyleaf; it's from the late 18th century. Husbandry has come on a bit since then.'

'Actually there was a far more interesting title, but it's on the highest shelf. I couldn't reach it, and the rolling library ladder has three rungs missing. I don't suppose you'd try reaching it for me?' Ophelia looked at Hamish expectantly. 'It's the thick blue leather bound, between the red and green.' She crossed her fingers behind her back, hoping he wouldn't realize what she was about.

'Title?' enquired Hamish, eyebrows rising.

'I couldn't quite make that out, but I'm sure it says "sheep" on the side.'

'Right…' said Hamish, stretching upwards. Despite his uncommon height, the top shelf was a good ten inches above his reach.

'I'll climb upon a seat,' suggested Ophelia, kicking off her little velvet shoes. 'Hold it steady for me.'

Hamish brought over the red plush chair from the centre desk. 'I suppose it better had be you,' he conceded. 'This might break if I try.'

Ophelia made a show of reaching for the shelf—encountering quite a lot of dust in the process and making herself sneeze.

It made her contrivance to make the chair wobble all the more convincing.

Pudding gave a warning yap.

'Steady there,' said Hamish, putting his hands to her hips.

Ophelia's pulse raced. Her dress, of terracotta coloured chiffon, was thin enough to let her feel the heat of his palms.

'I can see the title fully now. I was mistaken. Not about sheep at all. Something in Latin.' Ophelia rubbed at her nose, which threatened another sneeze, and hoped she wouldn't be struck down for telling lies.

She turned to find him gazing at her with unmistakable humour.

'Best get you down before you find any more irresistible books on the upper shelves to investigate.'

It struck her at that moment what had been apparent since their first meeting. He was devilishly handsome, he was strong, and he was decent.

Hamish's hands moved to her waist and lifted her down, gently and slowly. Her body, as if weightless, slipped down past his, chin to chin, and then chest to chest, until her toes touched the floor. There was no more than a hand's width between them.

She tilted back her head and, without the least hesitation, welcomed his lips upon her own.

Looking back, Ophelia could not have said whether it was she who kissed Hamish or whether his mouth first moved to hers. Whichever were true, it was the most natural of actions. She surrendered herself, Hamish's arms wrapping her close. When they parted, Ophelia was flushed and breathless. This was the kiss she'd been looking for.

It's like diving into a dark, velvet place and never wanting to come out, she thought.

She moved to kiss him again, but he stepped back.

He spoke with obvious reluctance. 'It's probably best if we don't.'

Ophelia endeavoured to keep her expression neutral. 'Oh, of course. There's a time and place for everything. Not very private here.'

His voice was a little ragged. 'It's not just that. You don't really know me. Whatever you think you're doing, it's not as simple as a kiss.'

Turning away, he prodded the fire with the poker, sending sparks up the chimney.

'Besides which, you're much younger than me,' he added brusquely. 'You know very little about the world. It wouldn't be right for us to start anything...to do anything.'

A strange constriction about Ophelia's ribs made it hard for her to speak. 'No need to explain,' she managed.

She bent to pick up Pudding, who gave her cheek a sympathetic lick. 'I understand completely. If you don't like me in that way it's absolutely fine. Better to be honest!'

She could see him attempting to find the right words, to soothe her or let her down gently. The thought of him pitying her was too much to bear.

'Think nothing of it,' she said firmly. 'Ridiculous of me. You're right. I hardly know you.'

It took every ounce of control for her to leave the room without him hearing her sob.

Retreating to the privacy of her bedroom, it was no comfort to see that she had a smear of grey dust over her cheek from touching the grubby shelves.

8

SPEAKING OUT

OPHELIA PUT ON HER MOTHER'S CRIMSON VELVET. IT WAS OPEN ACROSS the shoulders and upper back, but vastly warmer than the gown she'd worn the previous evening. Dampening her curls a little, she coaxed them into shape on either side.

She was determined to demonstrate to Hamish that she was a woman of the world—an attractive, mature woman, able to rise above their kiss in the library. It was a passing impulse that meant nothing.

They were joined at dinner by spinster cousins of the family Evelyn and Alice, the reverend of the local kirk, a sprinkling of respectable neighbours, and Colonel Faversham, who'd served with Morag's husband years ago.

Ophelia had known his type as soon as she'd laid eyes on him—a member of the bottom-pinching brigade. No female posterior would be safe.

Colonel Faversham was known for his glass eye, the original having been lost during the Second Anglo-Boer War. At moments of extreme passion (such as in the heat of debate at the House of Lords) it was prone to expel itself. Hostesses in town and country went to some lengths to avoid him becoming overexcited, lest the eye pop out and journey unwanted amongst the condiments.

In fact this was his second, the first having been propelled into the path of the leading horse at Ascot, and kicked by its hooves into the crowd, never to be seen again. It had not prevented the filly from romping to unexpected victory, at odds of 120-1. The Colonel had used his winnings to pay for an upgrade. In a startling shade of green, he believed the eye was a great improvement on nature.

Colonel Faversham addressed Ophelia over a fork of roast goose with chestnut stuffing. 'Now young lady. Nice looking gal like you oughtn't to be single; too much temptation to fall into wicked ways. Don't deny it! I know the urges of the young. Best put a husband in your bed!'

'Lascivious swine!' grumbled Ebenezer.

Ophelia felt a surge of warmth towards him.

The Colonel's luxuriant eyebrows wiggled provocatively. 'Don't you agree, Vicar?' He jabbed a conspiratorial elbow at his dining companion.

Reverend McAdam looked most alarmed. Of the Presbyterian faith, the abundant charms of Mrs. McAdam had warmed his marital bed for nigh on forty years. The Colonel's remark was impertinent.

Ophelia's gaze drifted relentlessly to Hamish, who sat at the far end of the table. He appeared to be hardly speaking tonight, as if wrapped in thoughts of his own.

Misses Evelyn and Alice Craigmore, meanwhile, were admiring the figure of the Colonel.

'Not bad for his age, Evelyn,' remarked Alice. 'Good teeth.'

As if on cue, the Colonel grinned in their general direction.

'Yes, he might do. Powerful stamina, I'd imagine,' replied her sister.

It was a game of theirs, to weigh up the merits of gentlemen as prospective husbands. They liked to be thorough in their examination. Most men, sadly, failed to meet their exacting standards.

They had lived their whole lives in respectable spinsterhood, at 17 Durness Walk, in the grand city of Aberdeen, and sixty-two years of spinsterhood quite spoils a woman since she is permitted indulgence of every fancy and finds herself much freer, in mind and body, than her married counterparts.

The sisters had never found a man (it had not occurred to them that, in fact, they might require two) worthy of their surrender. However, the Colonel was scoring highly.

'One can sense some men's enthusiasm,' noted Alice. 'He'd be like a terrier down a rabbit hole.'

'Dreadful you!' exclaimed Evelyn, giggling into her napkin.

Ophelia wondered if the spinsters realized their supposedly private conversation was perfectly audible to others around them.

The Colonel turned the conversation to politics, remarking to Ophelia his surprise at her father's recent support of the women's cause.

Ophelia was always ready to defend her father's liberal leanings. 'Daddy is quite forward-thinking. He's always been in favour of women's suffrage.'

'With all women over the age of twenty-one now voting, we've added five million to the electoral roll. We may outnumber the men at the next election,' stressed Enid.

'I'll drink to that,' proclaimed Constance, raising her glass.

'Poppycock!' spluttered Ebenezer, 'Women are physically, mentally and morally inferior to men. Canne be trusted to vote! They should be at home, raising their bairns. Leave politics to the men, eh Hamish?'

Before Hamish had a chance to reply, Morag intervened. 'Really, Ebenezer, we are not utterly incapable of understanding the issues of the day, despite our late Queen Victoria's thoughts on the matter. I too was a Suffragist, in my younger days.'

'Quite so!' affirmed Ophelia. 'Look at Lady Astor, taking her place in the House, and Margaret Bonfield. Who knows what they, and other women, might achieve? We could soon have women serving on the cabinet, or even as Prime Minister!'

She heard Ebenezer snort and mutter but found herself suddenly animated. She'd had no idea that her grandmother had been active in promoting votes for women. Her mother's support for the movement had been more in thought than in deed; Ophelia couldn't imagine Lady Finchingfield chaining herself to railings.

She urged, 'Women do need to be heard. My father voted for the Women's Employment Act too; it's a travesty that marrying precludes so many women from working. Can our lives have purpose in simply looking after a husband? It's abominable that it didn't pass the House.'

Looking the length of the table she saw Hamish's eyes intently upon her, as if seeing something for the first time. Her heart, which she'd been trying so hard to retain control of, trembled.

Several conversations erupted, everyone now having an opinion to contribute.

Fortified by alcohol, and a wink from Launcelot, Ophelia revealed most loudly, 'I've been reading Radclyffe Hall's *Well of Loneliness*. They're saying that she'll be tried for obscenity, just for writing about women falling in love with other women. Where's the freedom if we can't even write what we like!'

Reverend McAdam looked most uncomfortable, but Morag came to Ophelia's aid.

'Sounds marvellous, my dear. Please do lend it to me. I'll pass along my Agatha Christie. It's *The Mystery of the Blue Train*, full of that funny Hercule Poirot. Ebenezer, you enjoy books about trains, don't you, darling?'

'Not ones with foreigners in 'em!' barked Ebenezer. 'And not novels either. Give me a proper book—one with facts, not fancies, and none of that smut!'

Constance remarked, with seeming innocence, 'Hamish has lent me *Lady Chatterley's Lover*. Would you believe, Mr. Lawrence's heroine bears my name. And he's quite right; woman cannot live for the mind alone. Love only ripens when body and mind are content.'

'Inferno of depravity,' muttered Ebenezer.

Enid chipped in, 'I keep trying to remember if Mr. Lawrence and I have ever met. He does seem to know women rather well...I've marked several passages in my own copy to return to.'

At the other end of the table, Hamish, apparently unafraid of ruffling feathers, also had an opinion to voice on the subject of Mr. Lawrence's scandalous book.

'He makes some interesting observations on the classes. Men are working in dangerous conditions, given less thought than we might to a dog. It's a travesty that the miners have been cut off from striking again. Every man deserves a fair wage and fair hours.'

This brought the Colonel's fist upon the table. 'No one in their right mind can have approved of the general strike. It brought the country to a standstill, all those men shirking their work.'

The Reverend nodded. 'I heard the Prime Minister on the radio, calling it an attack on Britain's democracy. We all have our duty. Must knuckle down, however hard the conditions, like we did in the war. More to living than personal comfort.'

The sentiment was somewhat spoilt by his helping himself to another portion of potatoes.

'Servants of Beelzebub!' grumbled Ebenezer, though at no one in particular, and without raising his head from the last scrapings of his mashed celeriac. He was obliged to eat most of food in pureed form these days, although he'd have loved a bit of grilled cutlet.

'Those blighters refusing to do their jobs,' continued the Colonel. 'They deserved a whipping! My valet did his part by driving a bus on his day off. Keeping the services going, you know, and what do you think happened? It was set on fire! There was fighting on the street, in Belgravia! Right under the drawing room windows! I leant out and poured water over them, but it didn't make the slightest bit of difference. Later, I saw a tank on the edge of St. James' Park. It was as if the world had gone mad.'

'Filthy swine!' gnashed Ebenezer. 'Derailing the Flying Scotsman was the last straw—fine engine that, work of craftsmanship. Ought to have arrested the bloody lot of them.'

'You can hardly lock up almost two million people,' pointed out Hamish.

～

Downstairs, in the kitchen, Mrs. Beesby plated up the Charlotte Russe, while Una and Jennet tackled the washing up.

'That looks right nice, Mrs. B,' remarked McFinn. 'What's the chances there'll be some left for us?'

'Don't hold your breath, but don't be worrying yourself either. I've a treacle pudding for us, wi' custard n'all. It'll be waiting once you've served the liqueurs. There's a good bit o' the goose remaining; I'll make us a stew tomorrow, wi' fresh bannocks.'

'You're a good'un, Mrs. B,' said McFinn.

'Aye, and Mr. Haddock will be giving your ear a clip if you don't take this tray up. Off with ye, and no sticking your thumb in for a taste.'

9

AN UNEXPECTED INHERITANCE

OPHELIA WOKE WITH THE FEELING THAT SHE HAD STARTED OFF VERY much on the wrong foot with Hamish and that she should certainly apologise. She was ashamed of herself. She'd been brought up with far better manners than she'd shown towards him.

As she reviewed moments from last night's dinner, she couldn't help but notice that she approved of many of Hamish's views and opinions. For all his infuriating ways, he was worthy of her respect. Moreover, she'd seen the way he'd looked at her.

She didn't know what had been getting into her lately. Just because she'd been sent away and was having to make the best of it in the Scottish wilds didn't mean that she should forget her manners.

Outside, the sun was shining and it looked to be a splendid day. Perfect for new beginnings!

She pulled on a simple tunic in lemon muslin and a cotton gauze cardigan. It was an outfit she'd chosen for herself, with daffodil yellow shoes to match and a silk scarf for her hair. She tied the scarf carefully, the bow under her left ear. Sensible, modest, yet becoming.

Ophelia went straight into breakfast but found it empty. It was far too early for the older ladies to be down, and Ebenezer was too creaky to take his anywhere but his bed.

She found Haddock and inquired after Hamish's whereabouts.

'He's taken the car m'lady and driven to Inverness, I believe, collecting guests for tonight's gathering.

Damn! She'd forgotten more guests were arriving. The castle would soon be brimming with bores.

She'd have to nab Hamish later. She could perhaps take him up on the offer of a spot of fishing, and who was to say that one thing might not lead to another. Some scruple had held him back when they'd kissed in the library, but she was confident of winning his affections.

That afternoon, while the spinster cousins took a nap, Ophelia joined Morag, Constance, and Enid for their customary afternoon tea. She'd found that their conversation tended to stray into areas wonderfully unconventional. Today, they were discussing past lovers. It seemed that Lady MacKintoch and Lady Devonly had enjoyed quite a few beaux before they married.

Aphrodite, Morag's aged Pekinese, was slumbering upon the sofa, head laid daintily upon a tasselled cushion.

'Oh, how sweet!' commented Ophelia. Pudding, in agreement, took a flying leap onto the divan, to place her own head upon the Pekinese, using her abundant belly as a pillow.

Aphrodite opened one eye and considered growling. However, a moment of inward debate settled the matter, she being a dog of sufficient brain to gauge priorities, and far too comfortable to expend the effort required to discourage the trespasser. Her eye swivelled in its socket but otherwise gave no indication of disapproval.

Morag sipped her tea thoughtfully. 'Sad, as one gets older, to think of all those one once kissed and danced with (before I married Angus of course). So many have fallen off the perch.' She helped herself to a shortbread biscuit. 'I've invited Ranulph to join us tonight. You remember him, Enid? He proposed to you before he ever did me. At the New Year's Eve Ball at the Savoy. Do you recall?'

'Ranulph Van Kloeper!' exclaimed Enid. 'Oh yes! I *do* remember. I wonder if he's still as handsome. No doubt he remains as rich. I saw one of his films a while back. Simply divine. *Samson and Delilah*, with his latest wife in the lead role.'

'I know the one,' added Constance. 'She was a showgirl, Loretta something. She has a charming smile, among her other charming assets.'

The three ladies tittered into their tea.

'I'd no idea he'd courted you, Morag,' added Constance. 'Just think, you could have become a Hollywood star. These directors are all the same, pushing their amours onto the silver screen.'

'I think that's rather what put me off,' admitted Morag. 'Far too many glittering stars in the constellation; a woman wants to feel that her husband has eyes only for her.'

Too right, thought Ophelia, *if I ever have a husband, I shall expect utter devotion. What point is there otherwise?*

Morag sipped her tea. 'The only other women in my Angus's life were those with four feet; he did love his dogs and horses.'

'Quite!' agreed Enid. 'For myself, I didn't take the proposal seriously. I think Ranulph propositioned at least four of us that night. I wonder what he'd have done if we'd all said yes!'

'I've invited Charles as well, although I fear he hasn't aged as well as Ranulph,' Morag went on. 'I do hope he still has his own teeth; he used to be a spectacular kisser.'

'Good old Chips—although he used to make the most bizarre noises at crucial moments.' Enid refilled their cups. 'He's a baronet now, you know.'

'Yes!' exclaimed Constance. 'I'd quite forgotten. We were behind the morning room curtains at the Marchioness of Pippsbury's, and I had to put my hand over his mouth or who knows who'd have come running.'

Ophelia listened in wide-eyed wonder. It didn't sound as if things had changed greatly since her grandmother had been a debutante— proclamations of love that amounted to very little, and illicit kisses (and much besides) when chaperones could be dodged.

Ophelia couldn't help but admire Morag's audacity. She'd no doubt that her grandmother had chosen to invite her old flames in the hope that they'd fight for her attention.

Still, if we can't do such things on our sixtieth birthday, when can we?

'I'm afraid that everything has been far too dull of late for you Ophelia,' said Morag. 'However, we'll have some young people at the party who I hope may amuse you. There's the Comte de Montefiore, whom you may find amusing, and his step-sister, Felicité. Their mother was a dear friend of Lady Devonly many years ago. We have hopes that, perhaps, there may yet be wedding bells in a certain quarter.'

She clapped her hands excitedly. 'They spent some days here in early spring, mostly riding. We're very fond of them.'

Wedding bells for who, exactly?

Ophelia put Pudding on her lap.

I expect the Comte will be a ghastly cad, wanting me to laugh at his awful jokes, and there will be constant pouncing. No doubt his sister will be frightful too, full of simpering. It'll be like London all over again.

Morag replaced her cup upon the table. 'Now, I must speak frankly to you, my dear, on serious matters. I know that your mother is keen to see you wed, as am I.' She looked Ophelia in the eye. 'I believe that a husband well-chosen can be a rock in this tumultuous sea of life. However, I would not have you marry the first titled half-wit who stumbles across you. I want you to choose carefully, finding your soul-mate. Then, you'll be as happy as Constance and I were in our marriages.'

Ophelia smiled warmly at her grandmother. It was good to know that someone was on her side.

'Moreover, I find that your mother is far too preoccupied with the "show" of things, rather than the substance. For this reason, I'm going to arrange that Castle Kintochlochie passes to you, Ophelia.'

Pudding, suddenly gripped very tightly, let out a yelp.

Morag went on. 'I hardly imagine that my daughter will want to live here. She never has liked the wilderness. No doubt, she expects you to feel the same, which is why she views sending you here as punishment.'

'I didn't expect to like it up here myself. But I truly do think it's beautiful,' said Ophelia, unable to hide her excitement.

'We love you, and would like you to make this your home,' urged Morag.

Constance dabbed at her eyes with her handkerchief. 'Oh yes, my dear. How lovely it would be to have you with us always.'

Morag sighed. 'Daphne would, under usual circumstances, have inherited the castle upon my death, although not the title—of course. There's no one for that to go to, since Teddy died, and there's no living male issue on Angus' side. That honour will fall to your own firstborn son.'

Her eyes sought out Ophelia's. 'I always regretted being blessed with just the two offspring myself, and thought it a shame that Daphne conceived but once; though a lovely "one" you are, my darling! However, the castle would come alive as home to a larger family.'

Ophelia's cheek warmed. She hadn't given much thought to becoming a mother, and certainly not to a hoard of children running about the place. Nonetheless, she silently vowed to prove herself worthy of the affection she received at Kintochlochie, and to live up to her grandmother's belief in her.

'You'll soon learn about the estate, Ophelia,' Morag asserted. 'Hamish is a marvellous manager, but there's much to be done for its upkeep. I believe you're sensible enough to learn, and to shoulder responsibilities.'

'Hear, hear,' said Enid, giving Ophelia an encouraging wink.

Morag continued. 'Hamish has calculated the extra labour we need, and how we can ensure that the land pays for itself. I'm hoping that you might make a team of the job, although I can't say how long he'll stay on. He may have other plans…'

Constance patted Ophelia's hand. 'He'll come into my money one day, and may want to strike out on his own rather than managing this out-of-the-way place. It's hard to know a man's intentions; I'm not sure my nephew knows them himself.'

Morag smiled. 'Whatever happens, I know you'll rise to the challenge on your own if it comes to it. Like myself, you are a graduate of Girton, and Girton girls are never daunted.'

Pudding found herself unceremoniously deposited on the rug as Ophelia embraced her grandmother.

10

TOO MANY BUBBLES

THE HOUSE WOULD SOON BE BURSTING AT THE SEAMS. OPHELIA HEARD tyres on the gravel and went to the bedroom window, looking down at the new guests—mainly an assortment of elderly military men and their vague-looking wives. Large bosoms and even larger stomachs.

Her grandmother had kindly offered to send Mary to help her dress but Ophelia preferred doing such things herself. As Ophelia had few jewels of her own, Morag had given something from her own box—a diamond clip for her granddaughter's hair. Ophelia brushed through her curls and managed a reasonable job of fastening the clip high on one side. It really was a most beautiful gift.

A familiar motor pulled up, and her heart skipped a beat. Hamish emerged from the driver's seat, looking dashing in his kilt and Bonnie Prince Charlie dinner jacket.

She watched as he moved to open the rear door. An attractive woman stepped out and took his hand, her hair white-blonde, wearing a silver coat. She was followed by a tall, slender man, with dark hair and a thick moustache.

Hamish kissed her not only on each cheek but on the lips. The woman placed her arm through his and they disappeared inside, laughing.

Ophelia's head grew hot. *He's supposed to be grieving, not galli-vanting about picking up women.*

She slicked rouge to her cheeks and gave herself a boldly painted lip. Her appearance was improved, but her eyes bore evidence of anguish, looking huger than ever in her pale face. She chose a favourite from her wardrobe, an ice-blue dress speckled in glass beads that would catch the light and sparkle as she danced. Her shoes were embellished with rhinestones at the heel. A sequinned band went some way to controlling her hair, with a silvered ostrich feather tucked on the same side as her grandmother's clip.

A knock at the door revealed Mary, carrying a sash. 'Her ladyship sent it for you to wear, m'lady.'

Sewn from MacKintoch tartan, in muddied shades of brown and green, it was unspeakably ugly. Ophelia took it from Mary with barely concealed horror.

In this age of rush and bustle, it may be that some of you are yet to visit the bonnie hills of Scotland; that you have never, perhaps, enjoyed a dram of true Highland whisky, as is known to delight every Scots-man's heart, or that you are yet to dance an eightsome reel at a tradi-tional Scottish cèilidh. Not all are so blessed.

Yet, I ask you to imagine the utter joy conjured from the hearts of men and women when all three of the above happily combine.

On this particular evening, in celebration of her birthday, Morag had gathered to her many of like mind.

The chandeliers looked particularly dazzling, having been taken down and each tiny piece polished. Meanwhile every candle was lit, casting light and shadow to dance over the dour ancestors, leaving them floating and flickering in the darkness.

Lanterns had been looped through the trees straddling the long driveway up to the castle, and timeless bagpipe melodies resonated through the Great Hall. The piper, in formal regalia, gave them the full benefit of his lungs.

As Ophelia descended the stairs, her thoughts turned again to the ancient Highlanders who'd once inhabited the castle. The feet of their ghosts would surely be gathering on the upper landing, summoned by the elemental call. They might already be peering down curiously upon the assembly.

Morag and Ebenezer had formed a greeting party just inside the main doors. Ophelia wondered if it were the first time that tartan had been paired with lamé, seeing Morag wearing a full-length gown in the ancestral fabric, partnered with a gold turban. A large topaz shone from the centre, making her look like a Scottish maharaja.

An impressive pile of gifts was growing on the centre table. Ophelia's had been the improvised wrapping of some of her own Penhaligon's soap.

She wandered through to the ballroom, where a violin trio played a rather jolly Scottish jig and guests had started to drift towards the buffet.

Pudding was already stationed beneath the heaving tables of food, in company with Rex—the Colonel's nutmeg-brown Labrador—as well as Aphrodite and Braveheart. It was surprising how many sausage rolls found their way onto the floor. Meanwhile, there were plenty of approaching ankles to sniff.

Ophelia spotted Hamish at the other end of the room, surrounded by a crowd of elderly female admirers. The beautiful woman from the car stood at his side, her lithe frame clothed in a diaphanous gown of rose-petal pink. Hamish, in kilted evening dress, was undeniably, devastatingly handsome. Ophelia resolved not to approach them. Hamish could seek her out if he wanted to.

Launcelot, seeing Ophelia alone, came over and kissed her on both cheeks.

'You look divine my darling, and, I would say, lowered the average age of the room a good ten years.'

'Well, it is Morag's shindig. You'd expect most of her friends to be of senior years,' replied Ophelia, searching the room for other young faces. 'But I know what you mean. It's as if some of them have climbed out of the crypt.'

'Ah! You have an admirer already sweet one—and not so very ancient,' said Launcelot, giving an inclination of his head.

Weaving through the throng, and clearly headed their way, was the man with the thick moustache whom Hamish had collected from Inverness. He had a particular Mediterranean air, darkly dangerous.

'Allow me to introduce myself. I am the Comte de Montefiore.' He gave a low bow, which Ophelia noticed, allowed him to pass very close to her bosom. 'But you may call me Guillaume.'

He lifted her hand briefly to his lips, letting his eyes linger over the rest of her.

'This is Mr. Buffington, our artist in residence, and I'm Ophelia, Morag's granddaughter. I've been here barely a fortnight, but I must say that it's breath-taking. The Highlands are so beautiful.' Ophelia was determined to be charming.

Moreover, she hoped Hamish might see them chatting and feel some degree of pique.

'I rather delight in the bustle and glamour of the city, its sparkling illuminations, and equally dazzling residents.' The Comte, clearly, placed himself among the latter. 'For me, Paris is everything a city should be. Rome and Florence make pardonable attempts. London does its best, being tolerable in fine weather. I fear the Scottish capital cannot compare as a city, and the Scottish landscape is merely to be endured.'

Ophelia was about to respond, wanting to know why the Comte bothered to visit Scotland at all. However, she was beaten to the mark by Launcelot.

'I find it inconceivable that any could be untouched by the tranquillity of a herd of grazing sheep or the subtle permutations of shade upon a heathered hillside. To my mind, such persons are to be pitied.'

The Comte's eyes gave a noticeable roll in his head, then turned to examining the manicured curve of his fingernails.

The vision in pink appeared at his side. 'Take no notice of my stepbrother. He believes sheep exist only to be served with a rich jus and a good merlot. I am Felicité. A pleasure to meet you.'

Ophelia found herself rather wrong-footed. She wished very much to dislike this French woman, but her manner was so open and disarming.

McFinn passed by, offering flutes of champagne.

Felicité took a glass and, in moving her arm, the strap of her gown fell from her shoulder. Slowly, she slid it back into position, letting her long fingers linger at her collarbone. She inclined herself slightly towards the young man balancing his tray of drinks and looked up at him momentarily. Ophelia could have sworn that the footman smirked in return. The two maintained eye-contact certainly longer than was seemly.

Admittedly, the footman was attractive in his way, with close-cropped blond hair above a solid neck and firm jaw. His shoulders were broad, filling his uniform. However, there was something in his pale blue eyes Ophelia found disconcerting—they were in some way unreadable, as if his outward, placid expression concealed a multitude of inner thoughts and judgements.

The moment passed, and Felicité turned once more to Ophelia and Launcelot.

'The castle is heavenly! *J'adore. Mais naturellement*, I await the nocturnal pastimes. As soon as the lights are out, I expect the men will be donning their dressing gowns and skulking down the corridors.'

Launcelot spluttered into his glass.

'There is amusement in variety, *non*?' Felicité raised an elegant eyebrow. 'Of course, you can never be sure who is doing the creeping. At the house of my dear *amie,* the Duchess of Collingford, a burglar made off with her tiara having been seen by a housemaid, no less. She thought him a bed-hopper of the night and raised no alarm.'

From across the room came a booming Texan voice. 'This is some swell place y'have here, Morag. You should open the doors to the paying public. You'd make a killing! Americans would lap it up. Make up some ghost stories, serve them your haggis and get Hamish to wander 'round in that kilt of his. They'll buckle at the knees for a look-see at *his* knees.'

Ranulph guffawed loudly at his own joke, looking around to make sure others had appreciated his humour.

'*Mon Dieu.* Who is it that Lady MacKintoch has invited to her home? Someone from the Wild West and his saloon good-time-girl.' Felicité gave a wry smile. 'There is no accounting for taste.'

Her eyes narrowed at the sight of Ranulph Van Kloeper, wearing upon his head what Ophelia believed was known as a Stetson. Loretta, by his side, had chosen flouncing purple taffeta with an inordinate number of bows, not only upon the sleeves but down the centre of the dress and about the hem. Her headband was plumed with several extravagant feathers.

Ranulph might be getting on in years but there was nothing wrong with his eyesight and he was soon making a beeline in their direction, Loretta doing her best to keep up.

'Well howdy, ladies,' began Ranulph.

'I've heard all about you Mr. Van Kloeper,' said Ophelia, wishing to jump in before Felicité uttered a scathing remark. 'My grandmother tells me that you're big in Hollywood.'

'Certainly am, and this here is Loretta, my wife. Your grandmother was my first true love, back in the days before I knew one end of a camera from another. It's a real pleasure to be seein' her again. Some women have ever-lastin' beauty, and she's one of 'em.'

'You're very welcome to our home,' answered Ophelia.

'Why thank you,' said Loretta. 'You just watch out, honey, or Ranulph'll be kidnapping you and shippin' you back to Hollywood with us. You're as sweet as a pocket of peas on a Sunday.'

'Too right I will. With those big ole peepers o'yours you'd light up the screen. Audiences would go for you in a big way I reckon. What d'ya think, Loretta? We'll make her blonde? Get her to lose a few pounds? She could be the next big thing!'

Felicité turned away but Ophelia could hear her laughter.

'You're really too kind.' Ophelia smiled through gritted teeth. 'Are you peckish? Please do sample the buffet. We have game from the estate, and an assortment of wonderful pastries. Our cook, Mrs. Beesby, really is tremendous.'

'I see now why women find it so difficult to keep their figures over here,' remarked Felicité. 'Always eating, and always the heavy pies and cakes.' She looked pointedly at Ophelia.

'The days of corsets are gone,' countered Ophelia. 'Our figures are our own now, and if it pleases us to eat a few buns, I say why not.'

She was rapidly revising her willingness to be fond of the French woman.

'Perhaps,' answered Felicité, 'but so much of what is served is a medley of animals—your pigeon, and partridge, venison, mutton, and rabbit. Is there any creature you do not put on the plate? Even your puddings are full of animal lard, such as your roly poly jam. *C'est horrible!'*

The music paused and Hamish rapped a spoon upon the side of a glass to bring hush. With help from Hamish, Morag climbed upon a footstool to give her address.

'My darlings,' she began. 'Thank you all for joining me this evening. I wish there to be no formalities. Enjoy yourself heartily. Our first dance is *Strip the Willow.* Find your partners, and take your places.'

Taking Hamish's hand, she settled into her place opposite, motioning others to join them.

Ophelia was just wondering if she might ask Launcelot to partner her when her arm was firmly grasped.

'You must be Ophelia! You're the spit of your grandmother from when she was a pretty young thing.' The man grinned, displaying rather uneven, yellow teeth, beneath a wild thatch of moustache. 'I'm Charles Chippington, but they all call me Chips.'

Despite his thinning grey locks and sagging cheeks, he had remarkable strength. There was no doubting his intention to lead her onto the dance floor.

'Oh…lovely,' Ophelia managed.

The music began and couples were soon twirling madly. Chips was certainly a keen partner. The pace of the dance was so fast that Ophelia had little opportunity to remove one wrinkled hand, straying where it should not, before the other eagerly found a place elsewhere upon her person.

She was relieved to pause for breath as they clapped the top couple down through the middle, before moving up the hall to take new places. She caught sight of Hamish, who was clearly getting into the swing of things. Ophelia's stomach tightened. He'd trimmed his beard since she'd last seen him, making the square of his jaw more apparent.

The dance was a whirlwind, and Ophelia spent so much effort preventing Chips' hands from straying inside her clothing that, by the time the final notes closed, she was quite dizzy. She gave a curtsey and staggered off, hoping to avoid any more immediate torture.

The old goat was not to be so easily deflected.

'You're as firm as a peach!' he said, giving such a gigantic, lecherous wink she thought he might topple over. He patted her bottom, steering her towards the buffet. 'Pork pie! That's what we need. Keep the strength up for another go!'

He bit enthusiastically into a pickled gherkin. 'If I were thirty years younger I'd propose on the spot. Lovely young filly! I'd find a place for you in my stable! Work up a sweat and then enjoy a jolly good rub down, eh!'

He winked again and gave Ophelia's rear a ferocious pinch.

'Dammit!' he grumbled. 'Think I've strained something. It's the groin! Old war wound. Plays up if I get too frisky. Might have to sit down.'

With a look of great disappointment, he limped away and Ophelia lost no time in removing herself. She took a glass of champagne and made a beeline for Enid, who was standing nearby.

'Do men ever become less of a handful?' She took a large swig.

'I can hardly call myself an expert,' admitted the novelist. 'I had my share of beaux in my day, but I soon decided that men were more bother than they were worth. I don't attempt to understand them, only to enjoy their physical charms when the mood takes me.'

Ophelia frowned. 'I sometimes think it's myself I don't understand.'

'Perfectly natural. Don't worry, dear. You'll work it out.' Enid patted her arm companionably.

Felicité glided up with Hamish in tow.

'You are the Ms. Ellingmore of the romantic novels, are you not?' asked Felicité. 'I read your *Desert Surrender*. Most thrilling.'

'Speaking of desert adventures, I caught *The Sheik* at the cinema years ago,' added Hamish. 'A bit over the top I thought—all that kidnapping and forced seduction. Funny how it captured something in the female imagination.'

'My Hamish! You have no idea! Valentino! *Mon Dieu*, how I cried the tears when he died,' lamented Felicité. 'My darling, you must be my Valentino, and I shall submit to you in all things.'

She raised his fingers to her lips and gave them a playful bite.

Hamish responded by kissing her forehead.

Ophelia looked away, feeling suddenly short of breath. She downed the rest of her glass and looked about for an escape.

Her tartan sash was suffocating her. She pulled it over her head, casting it behind her.

On the dance floor, people were gathering for a reel. Despite having no partner, Ophelia came forward, weaving between shoulders. Someone took her hand and found a place for her.

The music began and she tried to keep up, but kept finding herself in a muddle.

'Wrong way,' hissed one of the women in her circle. The gentleman to her right, a pleasant-looking chap with blond hair, adjusted her as best he could, smiling benignly.

'Your turn in the centre,' he whispered, nudging her forward.

The champagne (had it been three glasses, or only two) had gone to her head. Giggling, Ophelia lifted her skirts and flung her legs high, then threw her arms over her head, clicking her fingers. She let out a large whoop to top it off, and then laughed some more. She was sure she'd seen someone do something similar. All rather absurd, but surprisingly fun.

'Good God,' said Hamish, watching from the side-lines. 'What *is* she doing?'

'I think there have been too many bubbles for her head,' mused Felicité.

'Goddarn it!' said the Texan. 'There's a woman who wants some attention.'

'It does look a hoot, honey,' giggled Loretta. 'I'm gonna join in.'

With that, she kicked off her shoes, and began a tipsy jig of her own, making Ranulph chuckle.

'*Mon Dieu*! Painted toenails!' remarked Felicité. 'Now I have seen it all.'

Ophelia had drunk far too much for her own good. Her high kicks were clearly evidence of that. Excusing herself from the circle, she stumbled out, past raucous laughter and jumping bodies, jostling backs and plates of food.

She exited across the Great Hall, seeking somewhere quiet, and found the drawing room.

I'll lie upon the sofa. Just for a bit, until my head stops spinning.
She dozed off, but was not long after awoken by a rattling sound.

'Damn arthritis!' cursed a familiar voice.

Ophelia opened an eye and saw Colonel Faversham at the foot of the divan. He was trying to open the pretty container that always sat on the side table nearest the fire, decorated with an image of the Isle of Skye. In fact, it was a tin designated for marrow-bone biscuits, although both Morag and Constance were more inclined to slip a buttered scone or some shortbread to the hairy faces that presented themselves for a treat.

Ophelia sat up. 'Here, let me,' she offered, taking it from him.

'Thank you, m'dear.'

He helped himself to a dog biscuit. 'Hmmm, not bad. Are they homemade?'

'No. Shop, I think,' answered Ophelia with a smile. 'Here, have another.'

'Don't mind if I do.' He found the drinks cabinet and poured them both a large whisky.

'Enjoying yourself?'

'I'm not sure,' said Ophelia, sniffing the proffered drink. It smelt strongly of peat. 'I'll decide later.'

The Colonel clinked his glass against hers. He was swaying a little. It clearly wasn't his first. He raised the glass in a toast. 'Here's to you, as good as you are, and here's to me, as bad as I am.'

'Hear, hear,' said Ophelia. The strangest things made sense once you'd had a few.

'*Slàinte mhath*, my dear.'

Nausea welled up and, anxious that she might vomit, Ophelia made for the French doors, out onto the terrace.

'This is the sixth tray of raspberry meringues I'm carrying up those stairs,' grumbled Maggie. 'Talk about the idle rich. I'll be rubbing my corns come bedtime.'

'Less of your moaning, Maggie,' chided Mrs. Beesby. 'We've spent the past week making this lot. At least it's appreciated. I'll venture that these guests havenae seen the likes of my choux puffs afore! Lady Morag'll see us right when all's done. There'll be a proper Christmas bonus I've nae doubt.'

McFinn, coming down the steps as Maggie passed upwards, gave her rump a slap. Wasn't it his duty to rally the spirits of the female staff, bestowing a playful pinch or a saucy squeeze? They rarely complained. They mightn't look like hothouse orchids (Maggie's moustache was more prominent than his own) but all flowers flourished with the right care. When he was butler—Haddock surely had no more than a few years left in him—McFinn would truly come into his own.

'Don't tell me that none o' those sweet things find their way into yer mouth.' McFinn grinned. 'Not that I'm complaining. I like a bit o' padding.'

'Cheeky sod!' retorted Maggie, straightening her skirt. She looked pleased nonetheless; if it wasn't for McFinn paying her the odd compliment there probably wouldn't be any. If he thought her posterior worthy of attention, she'd enjoy the moment.

Mrs. Beesby saw his high jinks in a different light. 'None of that, ye saucy kipper!' Her ladle caught him a rap across the knuckles. 'Get this lobster mayonnaise up there afore it curdles.'

11

SPARKLING AND ENCHANTED

H AVING RELIEVED HER STOMACH OF SOME MEASURE OF THE troublesome cocktail of whisky and champagne, Ophelia gulped down the night air, so refreshingly cool.

Her arms, being bare, were goose-bumped, and she shivered as she stood on the terrace. In front of her the loch's surface shimmered, bathed in that light by which owls hunt.

From behind her where the windows threw shafts of gold onto the dark gravel, a voice, low and soft and lilting, said, 'You should see it in winter. The frost comes in the night, glazing the ferns and the bracken. The loch's like misted glass.'

She didn't need to turn. She knew who it was.

'I was looking from the library window when you stepped outside. It's too chill to be out here in that dress.' The pale chiffon blew lightly in the breeze as Hamish placed something around her shoulders; it looked like a wrap of Morag's.

Ophelia tipped back her head, dazzled by the stars filling the sky. 'The moon is like a keyhole, don't you think? Leading somewhere sparkling and enchanted. That's where I want to go!'

Hamish laughed. 'I've come to tell you off for drinking too much, but I think I might like you like this.'

'I can't help being me,' said Ophelia, feeling an urge to let things tumble out. 'I want to gallop rather than trot, and to dance how I like, and with whom I like, and to speak my mind, and to look at the moon in the middle of the night, and...to be held, and loved, and...kissed!'

'You are a strange creature...there's something...' His voice trailed off.

'Oh Hamish, I had some whisky and it's gone right to my toes! I'm wobbly all over. Why don't you take me upstairs and tuck me into bed?'

He leant in towards her so that she became aware of the warmth of his body. Her knees weakened and a wave of lust tugged between her legs. When his kiss came it was slow and tender. He cradled her head gently as she leaned back, raising her face to him.

She sunk into the dark, magical delight of his mouth on hers, and the smell of him—like wood ash and pine. She thought he tasted of peat, but perhaps it was the smoky whisky lingering on her own tongue.

At last, he lifted his lips from hers but held Ophelia still, looking at her through lids half closed.

From the ballroom she heard a burst of laughter, and the music starting up for a new dance. She remembered who was waiting there, who might be watching them even at that moment.

Ophelia wriggled away. 'I want to but it's not right. I don't know what she is to you, but she's something, this Felicité. I may not like her very much but I won't carry on with you behind her back.'

Ducking from his embrace, she ran inside.

12

A GOOD TIME HAD BY ALL

Ophelia wasn't the only one who'd been liberally enjoying the hospitality of her hostess. The party was looking more convivial by the minute. Inhibitions were obviously going out of fashion.

As she squeezed past assorted bodies, several hands made a grab for her. She spotted old Chips chatting up Constance to one side, and the Colonel making eyes at Enid on the other. When Ophelia reached the Great Hall, she found Ranulph tangoing with Loretta, who seemed to have lost not only her shoes but all her feathers.

'Dip me, baby, dip me,' she was saying, her voice husky, and her leg flipping onto Ranulph's shoulder.

Ophelia's head was swimming. All she wanted was to climb the stairs and collapse into bed. She was about halfway up when there was a screech of 'Sardines' from the ballroom. Ophelia pressed herself against the wall as a crowd of over-excited revellers thundered by, no doubt heading for the wing of guest bedrooms. It seemed that age and dignity did not always go hand in hand.

She'd barely reached the top of the stairs when she heard Chips cooing to her from behind. In a panic, she dived through the nearest door and found herself in a small, dark space—the linen cupboard.

At least it was warm!

He stumbled past, still calling for her. She'd leave it a minute and then see if the coast was clear.

Ophelia skimmed her hands over the walls either side of the door but couldn't find a switch.

She wasn't bothered by the thought of spiders, or mice, or whatever other creatures tended to lurk in dark cupboards but after some moments, she thought she heard something breathing, very close.

Suddenly, a moustache tickled her.

Hot breath landed on her neck, and fingers crept around her waist. The thing in the cupboard spoke.

'Hello, little rabbit.' It brought its mouth closer to her ear. 'Like Valentino in *The Sheik,* I have kidnapped you. We are in the desert, in my Bedouin tent. You struggle, yet it is hopeless. You are in my power, and I will do unspeakable things to you.'

Ophelia gave a sigh and extended her elbow sharply into the thing's ribs, extracting an 'oomph' from her would-be lover.

'We aren't in the desert. We're in a cupboard. And I can assure you that any unspeakable things will be conducted at my will, not in spite of it!' She gave the door a push but it refused to budge.

'Do not fight it, *ma chérie.*' The Comte, though slightly breathless, was nothing if not determined. Despite the limited space, he managed to push his leg between hers. 'It is the fantasy of all sweet English maidens to be ravished by French aristocracy, is it not?'

Ophelia gave the door a solid kick and it flew open, tumbling her into the corridor. At that moment, who should be passing but Hamish, with Felicité upon his arm.

As her step-brother emerged from the recess, Hamish's expression darkened.

'Do not mind us, *ma chère.*' Felicité waved her hand. 'We do not spoil the fun of others.' She smirked. 'But are there not enough bedrooms? Do you need to resort to linen cupboards?'

Felicité pressed herself proprietorially to Hamish's chest, her long fingers coaxing open the buttons of his jacket. 'You were seeing me to my room, Hamish. We need not linger here in draughty corridors when a warm bed is waiting.'

Hamish allowed himself to be guided away, and it was Felicité who looked back over her shoulder and kissed her fingers in farewell. Ophelia heard soft laughter as Hamish opened the door, and the two moved within.

~

'Disgraceful I call it,' grumbled Maggie. 'It's like musical beds up there. I hardly dare think what state the sheets'll be in. Me and Nessa'll be hours putting them through the wringer.'

'They may be knocking on in years but they know how to enjoy themselves all right!' admitted McFinn. 'Putting the booze away too. Most wouldnae be able to find their own rooms if they wanted to. Mr. Haddock's sent me to bring up more Moët.'

'Never mind champagne. I'd settle for a nice cup of Ovaltine and my head on the pillow,' said Maggie.

'Too right,' agreed Jennet, running her finger around the edge of the trifle bowl before lowering it into the sink.

'I know whose pillow I'd like to get my head on,' grinned McFinn. 'Ooh la la and all that. Bet she's got a few tricks up her sleeve.'

'All flash!' sniffed Maggie. 'Silver fox fur and no knickers!'

'It's been a goodly time coming,' said Mrs. Beesby. 'Mr. Munro has been too long wi'out a wife. No man should be left lonely in his bed of a night.'

No one could disagree. As for little Una, the scullery maid, she sighed forlornly and continued scrubbing the pans. She'd keep Mr. Munro's bed warm anytime he liked, with or without a wedding ring on her finger.

13

A MISTAKE

THE HOUSE REMAINED SUBDUED UNTIL VERY LATE THE NEXT MORNING. Only two guests appeared at the eight o'clock breakfast table—stalwarts able to stomach their victuals regardless of alcohol imbibed in the hours previous.

Lord and Lady Faucett-Plumbly were unaccustomed to remaining in their bed beyond half past seven, regardless of the season, weather, or constitution (at least it had been so for Lord Faucett-Plumbly since the happy day upon which his marriage vows were sealed).

Having fortified herself with two slices of ham, five of Mrs. Beesby's venison sausages, three halves of sautéed tomato, and a large spoonful of scrambled egg, Lady Faucett-Plumbly looked about for further nourishment. These country visits did inspire the appetite.

'Arthur, would you fetch some porridge?' she asked.

'Of course, dear.'

It mattered not that his own egg was only half consumed and his sausages yet to be touched at all. Lord Faucett-Plumbly was aware of his spousal duty.

A bowl of steaming porridge was placed before his charming wife.

'Oh, really Arthur! You're hopeless. I don't know why I ask you to do anything at all!'

'Sorry, dear, have I forgotten something?' Lord Faucett-Plumbly knew it was easier to admit fault directly.

'Yes! You have, you silly man. With what should I eat this porridge?'

'A spoon, of course, my dearest.' He rose to fetch the cutlery.

Arthur was, at last, permitted to continue with his egg, though it had formed a rather unattractive skin while waiting for his return.

'Oh, vile!' spluttered Lady Faucett-Plumbly.

Her husband's fork paused in mid-air.

'Take this away. It's not right at all. Far too much salt!'

Lord Faucett-Plumbly, in a moment of daring, attempted a suggestion. 'My dearest, why not add some cream and see if it renders the recipe more palatable.'

'Don't start, Arthur!' barked Lady Faucett-Plumbly. 'If I say the porridge is inedible then that is what it is!'

'Is there anything else I might get for you, dear one?'

'I wouldn't mind another sausage, but I fear you greedily took the last from the dish. It would be a small gesture to offer it to me. However, I know you think only of yourself.'

'Not at all, my dove.' It pained him to do so, but there seemed no other path. No doubt, the hot dishes would soon be replenished.

Lady Faucett-Plumbly speared not one but two of the sausages from her husband's plate. 'You need to watch your waistline Arthur. One sausage is quite enough for a man of your age and disposition.'

'No doubt you're right, my love. You usually are.'

She eyed him suspiciously. 'I do hope that is not an attempt at humour, Arthur, or worse, sarcasm.'

McFinn entered with more steaming dishes, laden not only with the finest sausages, but with gammon and kedgeree.

'Jolly good!' said Lord Faucett-Plumbly, rising to fill his plate.

'No time, Arthur,' countered his wife, dabbing her mouth with her napkin and placing down her knife and fork with finality. 'I have a fourteen-mile hike planned for us and we must begin immediately, or we may miss lunch. I require little sustenance, as you know, but regular meals should be observed, for the sake of the digestion.'

Arthur paused, looking with longing at the newly arrived delicacies.

'Chop, chop!' countered his wife. 'Alas, what it is to be married to a man who thinks only of his stomach!'

The day passed lazily. By eleven, people had ventured forth in search of comfort. Emerson's Bromo-Selters were distributed, and Lady MacKintoch requested jugs of buttermilk laced with salt and pepper, swearing by it as the best cure for over-indulgence.

Ranulph had his own ideas. 'Raw egg, Tabasco, and vinegar; it's the only way to go, Morag, honey.'

'Here is an American idea I can approve of,' admitted the Comte. 'Add a splash of vodka and tomato juice and I shall join you.'

'Chin chin to that!' said Enid, whose own head was throbbing. She'd been most dreadfully forward with the Colonel and had woken in his bed around six that morning— to his snoring, and that of Rex, whose head lay between them on the pillows.

By the time the Faucett-Plumblys returned to the castle, Ebenezer had broken out his homemade liqueurs and the house party was, once more, well on its way to companionable oblivion.

They'd drunk dry Ebenezer's 1923 batch of turnip and blackberry brandy and were starting on an experimental bottling of radish and rhubarb gin when Ophelia entered. She'd put off coming down for as long as possible, but the desire for food had finally overwhelmed her, and none of the staff seemed to be answering bedroom bells. No doubt, they had their work cut out for them without running up the stairs with trays.

Having had sufficient time to reflect on the events of the party and the state of her own feelings, Ophelia was determined to rise above petty jealousies. She would befriend Felicité and wish her, and Hamish, every happiness.

She saw them from across the room lounged upon a sofa, Felicité blowing a teasing kiss into the auburn curls at Hamish's neck. Still wearing his kilt, and with legs planted apart in manly fashion, he seemed more than content at the placement of her hand several inches above his bare knee.

On Ophelia's approach, he did shift in his seat a little and had the grace to look uncomfortable.

Pudding, trotting at Ophelia's heels, spotted Hamish's sporran and vaulted gleefully onto his lap. Her aim was true and she set about befriending the strange creature.

'She's very affectionate,' said Ophelia.

Pudding, held aloft by Hamish, gave his face a lick.

Lady Faucett-Plumbly took a chair nearby. 'Dogs do not belong on furniture!' she admonished, raising a glass of something tinged a murky green to her lips.

Pudding was known for the shrillness of her yap, delivered when the humans about her were most unsuspecting. How many cups of tea had been flung into the air at her command, and how many cream-laden scones? Pudding's timing was impeccable.

No sooner was she placed upon the floor by Hamish than the terrier leapt towards Lady Faucett-Plumbly, uttering a canine volley of disapproval. One glass of sprout and nettle wine was cast to the skies. Following the rules of gravity, it then spattered upon Lady Faucett-Plumbly's tea dress, newly changed into from her walking tweeds.

Lady Faucett-Plumbly turned a shocking shade of purple.

'How unfortunate,' said Felicité. 'Still, there is always the silver lining. Now, you may throw away this horrible dress and wear something not like the curtains.'

She patted Hamish's exposed leg. 'Come, mon chéri. Let us take a walk in the fresh air and work up appetites for returning to bed.'

At dinner that night, despite wearing another of the sumptuous gowns left behind by her mother, full-length emerald silk, Ophelia felt her vitality being sucked away—much like the mulligatawny soup being slurped into the quivering mouths of the sea of ancients occupying most seats at her end of the table.

The candles lit down the centre caused the glassware to sparkle, reflecting a hundred flames. It should have seemed beautiful but only made her muse on the fleeting nature of happiness—glowing one minute, snuffed out the next.

Farther down she could see Felicité flirting with Hamish, first whispering in his ear and then, Ophelia could have sworn, darting her tongue to his lobe. Her dress, of sheerest nude chiffon, was beaded so low on the bodice that the full curve of her breasts was visible. One jiggle would have her nipples playing peek-a-boo.

'No better than dogs,' she heard Ebenezer mutter, to her right, seeing Hamish place a kiss upon Felicité's shoulder.

The Comte, it seemed, had decided to ignore Ophelia's rebuff in the linen cupboard. He nodded at Lady Faucett-Plumbly, and at her spouse—digging into his lamb chop with gusto, and leaned in to whisper to Ophelia, in a manner more intimate than she would have wished.

'There is a lot to be said for physical allure. If a woman cultivates the sexual appeal of a parsnip, she will find herself bedding a cabbage.'

'I'm sure they're both perfectly lovely, and deliriously happy,' Ophelia snapped, adding, 'In their own way.' Of course, she didn't believe so for a moment, but to agree with the Comte would be disloyal to her sex.

Felicité was whispering to Hamish, allowing her hair to brush his face. Ophelia saw him turn and smile.

Hussy! thought Ophelia. Never had she been thrown into such a paroxysm of jealousy; it was too sick-inducing. She took her glass and emptied it in three gulps. None of the dry sticks surrounding her seemed to notice. Haddock, however, appeared over her shoulder, to refill.

Resentment gnawed at her.

'I see who you are watching. The ring is almost upon the finger, I believe.' The Comte's voice was cool.

Ophelia's throat tightened but she retorted, 'I've no ambition in that direction; to marry is to become an exhibit. If your step-sister wants him she's welcome.'

Ophelia glared and took another swig of Pouilly-Fumé.

Meanwhile, the Comte's fingers lifted her skirt beneath the table, warm on her knee, then climbed to the top of her stocking. He hooked them under the garter.

'I do believe, my little rose, that, given half the chance, you'd have every man line up to kiss your bloomers.' His hand crept higher still, reaching the soft inner flesh of her thigh.

'Your whispered indecencies are nothing but hot air,' Ophelia hissed, endeavouring to remove the offending hand without causing a stir. She contemplated sticking her fork into it.

Recalling some gossip exchanged between her grandmother and Enid the day before, she added, 'If I'm not mistaken, your wife spends most of the year between Monaco and Milan, having found attractions elsewhere.'

The Comte withdrew his hand and his eyes flashed a little. He shrugged before picking up his own glass.

Ophelia let herself tune in to Ranulph, who was telling tales of Hollywood indiscretions and the vices of the stars. His voice broke across the chatter of the table. 'Felicité, I bet you're a fan of the new talking films. Tell us what you think.'

'I have seen *The Jazz Singer*, with Monsieur Al Jolson, six times,' she declared. 'And this Louise Brooks, they say she posed for a photograph without her clothes, and that she has kissed the belle Garbo. My secret wish is to be like the great Greta. Like me, she speaks little English, but she says all with her eyes, commanding the men to fall at her feet. She is mysterious and alluring, is she not?'

Her lashes fluttered wildly at Hamish. Ophelia didn't for a minute believe they were real.

Felicité continued to babble on. '*J'adore* Mademoiselle Clara Bow. Your Ophelia looks like her, does she not, with her head of curls?'

Ophelia was loath to acknowledge the compliment. She turned away, only to catch the eye of the Comte, filled with a certain malicious glitter.

Mrs. Beesby had again been working like a trouper, presenting a menu of ten courses. Ophelia watched as guests filled their stomachs—with filet of sole, with a terrine of ham hock, with quails in rosemary sauce, with poached salmon and Chatouillard potatoes, ox tongue pâté, and Russian salad.

She hardly ate two bites, her gaze relentlessly upon Hamish and Felicité. Meanwhile, the Comte continued to proposition her with increasingly vulgar scenarios.

None noticed her distress, not even Launcelot, who was deep in conversation with the Misses Craigmores.

Over the chocolate bavarois, Hamish rose from his seat and proposed a toast. 'We're gathered here to celebrate the sixtieth birthday of our beloved Lady MacKintoch. Let us raise our glasses to a life well-lived, a life of love and adventure. May we all be so fortunate.'

Having touched his glass to Morag's, he looked down fondly at the fair head of Felicité. As glasses were raised in response, she leapt up, gasping, '*Mon Cœur! Mon Ange!*' and took a kiss from him, full on the lips.

A wave of heat passed over her, and Ophelia feared she might faint. She stumbled from the table, caring not for manners, and fled to the conservatory where the windows were left ajar in the summer months.

Hamish isn't mine. He never has been and he never will be. He belongs to this Felicité. He loves her.

The room smelt over-sweet, of jasmine and honeysuckle, begonias and orchids, but the cool air revived her a little. She leaned out and breathed deeply, trying to calm her pulse, battling the pricking of her tears.

At last, she heard a footstep. She turned, thinking that perhaps Hamish had come to find her. He must, surely! He needed to tell her that it had all been acting; that it was her for whom he had feelings.

However, it was the Comte, removing his tie and dinner jacket, throwing them carelessly over a table of geraniums. He was holding a glass of brandy.

Her heart plummeted.

She turned to leave, but he grasped her wrist firmly and brought his face close to hers, his breath sour with cigar smoke.

A wave of nausea swept over her again but she held still as he kissed her, teeth raking her lips.

Voices drifted out to them, seemingly from the library, that of Felicité laughing and of Hamish. She heard a heavily accented voice, laced with coquetry. '*Vraiment!* This colonel is telling me that my beautiful Paris is *rempli* with pots of flesh!'

'Fleshpots, Felicité,' corrected Hamish. 'No doubt the old bugger is well familiar with them.'

Ophelia was brought back to the moment by the Comte giving her a savage nip, then growling in her ear. 'Don't lie to yourself. I know what it is that you want.'

Why not lose myself in this for its own sake, and forget Hamish, thought Ophelia. *Falling in love is nothing but poison.*

'You wish me to tear you, little rose, to pluck off your petals and crush them. Women have many secrets, but yours are not so difficult to read.'

It would serve Hamish right to come in and catch us, thought Ophelia.

'If you've something to show me, jolly well get on with it, or are you all talk?'

And with that, she discovered that there is only the thinnest of divides between what we want and what we fear, and the two often intersect. All that happened next, she thought later, occurred as if she were watching herself from a distance.

He knelt and raised her skirt, passing it over his head, so that he quite disappeared beneath. His fingers took down her French knickers, letting them drop to her ankles, and his mouth pressed warm to her belly.

His lips moved lower, breath hot against her sex, his moustache brushing against her fur. His hands reached around to cup her buttocks.

His voice was a low murmur. 'What sort of girl invites a man she has only just met to behave in this manner? A very wicked one, I think.'

Bastard! thought Ophelia, but whatever snake resided in her womb unfurled and shivered.

'You are impatient,' whispered the Comte.

She grasped at his head, urging him to proceed, raising her leg, eager for his tongue.

He laughed then, knowing that he had conquered her. So the hunter greedily consumes its prey; too late for the bird to take wing and evade capture.

Steps crossed the library. Had Ophelia's ears not been filled with her own ragged breath, and the thud of her heart, she would have heard the click of the door.

14

A MOMENT OF IMPULSE

THE MAIN EVENTS OF CELEBRATION HAVING BEEN CONCLUDED, MOST guests breakfasted promptly wishing to motor home, leaving only a handful of Morag's circle—Texan Ranulph and his wife Loretta, Enid and the Colonel, Felicité and the Comte among them.

Ophelia chose to lie late abed. She thought of the liberties she had allowed the Comte. It was dreadful, and glorious, and she hated him, and wanted him to do it again.

She had lain awake for hours, wracked with an awful headache and tumultuous feelings of shame and intoxication. If the world at large were to offer its moral judgement, it would surely have something to say.

Ophelia scrutinised herself in the mirror. *I'm corrupted and unable to be what I was before,* she thought, but her reflection looked just the same, if rather weary.

I'm trying on versions of myself, she concluded, *to see how they fit. Aren't I doing just as I planned, exploring what it means to be a woman, without becoming a dreary wife?*

She supposed she was, but, somehow, she did not feel satisfied.

~

At last, coming downstairs, she found Hamish and Felicité with the Comte, discussing plans for a trip to Edinburgh.

'*Délicieux!*' Felicité clapped her hands girlishly. 'I would so adore to see the upper apartments at Holyrood Palace. Perhaps we shall encounter the ghost of poor Rizzio, and see that mysterious bloodstain which refuses to be scrubbed clean? Fifty-six stabbings! *Mon Dieu! C'est horrible!*'

'*Bonne idée chérie,*' asserted the Comte. 'And perhaps petite Ophelia will come too. There is space in the car, is there not Hamish? And the Caledonian Hotel will have room for us all?'

By the glint in his villainous eye and the twitch of his moustache, the Comte's intentions were clear. Ophelia's heart thudded in response but, on reflection, sharing his bed did not appeal to her.

Meanwhile, the thought of watching Felicité and Hamish swooning over each other was more than she could bear. Let his fancy piece place her hand on his knee, or wherever else she liked; Ophelia wouldn't be there to see it.

Hamish did not give her the opportunity to answer. 'Ophelia is here to spend time with Lady MacKintoch. It would be unfair of us to deprive our hostess. From what I've seen, Ophelia is most accommodating to others. You would agree, no doubt, having last night received a tour of the conservatory in her capable hands.'

He looked pointedly at Ophelia and her face burned.

The Frenchman, caddish to the last, slipped a hand onto her bottom. Really! It was the assumption of consent she minded more than anything.

The three took their leave, Hamish refusing to speak directly to Ophelia, and Felicité in a flurry of extravagant cheek kissing.

Detestable creature! She's pure varnish; nothing of substance... Ophelia seethed. *And Hamish is simply foul. Has he no decent feeling?*

Deciding that the only thing liable to soothe her temper was a brisk outing across the hillside, Ophelia put on her stout shoes and a sensible costume for walking. Pudding, having eaten an excess of puff pastry, was less enthusiastic, choosing to bury her head under her mistress' pillow.

In fact, Ophelia had gotten no farther than the first bend in the driveway before a honking motorcar came barrelling up at speed, spraying gravel as it braked, and only narrowly missing her toes.

'Mind the bloody hell what you're doing!' she shouted, not caring if the driver were the Prince of Wales himself.

'Dash it! I do apologise,' said the man behind the wheel, raising his goggles and taking off his racing cap. 'Far too excited. Wanted you to see my new Green label, and here I go nearly knocking you over. Isn't she a beauty!'

Ophelia searched her memory for his face. He looked familiar but she couldn't place him. Someone from London? Not a friend of Percival's, she hoped. He was very blond and smooth-faced. He didn't look a day over eighteen.

Her confusion must have been obvious, for the young man exclaimed, 'It's me! Peregrine! You remember...or perhaps you don't. We were dancing a reel, and you were a bit unsure of the steps. I've not laughed so much in ages...although not at you of course. Well, perhaps a bit. Dash it! I mean to say, your dancing was a treat, especially when you took the centre.'

He was blushing now and Ophelia couldn't help but smile at his candidness.

'I tried to find you afterwards,' he went on. 'I looked all over, but you'd disappeared. Then people were playing that silly game, hiding behind curtains and what not. Someone grabbed me and we ended up sitting under the buffet table with some dogs. Too ridiculous!'

He paused for breath, but only briefly. 'Anyway, here I am. I wanted to come back yesterday, but the motor had a flat tyre and I had to get it fixed. I'm a good seven miles away, staying in a lodge with my parents for the summer, although they're in Aberdeen at the moment, visiting someone or other.'

'All right then.' Ophelia flipped her legs over to climb into the passenger seat. 'I'm game.'

'Top hole!' proclaimed the young man and, with wheels spinning, hit the accelerator.

It turned out to be the perfect tonic. The sun blazed overhead warming Ophelia's face. Neither of them spoke, Peregrine concentrating on navigating the bends of the steep road up, out of the glen, and then whisking them through woodlands, alongside the river and beyond. They drove for a good half hour before he slowed the car and pulled over at a high spot.

Peregrine jumped up to sit on the back of the seat and motioned for Ophelia to do the same. They both took off their jackets, revelling in the sunshine, and the view.

'Jolly good countryside they have up here!' Peregrine's hair, escaping from the sides of the leather cap, was very curly, rather like Ophelia's.

Hers, despite being under a little woollen beret, was a mass of tangles from having been blown about, but she didn't care. It had been exhilarating. Fleetingly, she thought of the other car journey, little more than a fortnight ago, when Hamish had picked her up from the station. It seemed like far longer.

Damn him! she thought. *I'm not wasting time pining for someone who's not interested.*

'What do you think of my Greenie?' asked Peregrine. '6.3:1 compression ratio, a four-speed gearbox, and she'll do 100mph on the flat. She can beat the Red or Blue labels into a cocked hat. I tell you, I could shake Mr. Walter Owen Bentley by the hand.'

Ophelia pushed off his cap and tucked a curl behind his ear. His eyes, true blue, looked straight into hers.

'Come here,' she said, and pulled him down into the seats.

Peregrine was an enthusiastic kisser—a little too keen perhaps, but not at all unpleasant. After a time, Ophelia guided him to her neck. She undid the buttons of her blouse and shrugged it down so he could kiss her shoulders too.

When his hands began to wander under her camisole, and to squeeze, she let him. He pushed the straps down, exposing her breasts. The sun was wonderful on her bare skin and it was thrilling to think that anyone might walk by, peer in, and see them.

She let his mouth kiss where she hadn't been kissed before and, all the while, a pulse throbbed between her legs. She'd only just met him, didn't know his family, or anything about him really, but that only made it more exciting. She'd imagined what the sex act would be like. She'd seen cows and sheep, and she'd read about it in an old farming manual years ago.

He paused, looking at her with flushed cheeks.

'I didn't expect...' he began. 'We were only going for a drive. But this is marvellous. You're marvellous.'

She took Peregrine's hand and guided it beneath her skirt. He was hesitant but she held his wrist, wanting him to carry on. Guiding him, she pushed his fingers where she wanted them to be.

Peregrine suddenly stopped, a look of panic on his face. 'Oh, Ophelia!'

She tensed, wondering if someone really was walking up the road and about to see them, but Peregrine wasn't looking up. His eyes were closed altogether, and he was biting his lip.

His body went rigid. 'I'm... I couldn't help it! I just couldn't!'

'Oh!' she exclaimed and then began to laugh.

Peregrine's groin, pressed to her hip, was damp.

'Don't worry,' she said, then apologized for laughing, and laughed some more.

'Dash it, Ophelia! A man's got his pride you know.' Peregrine sat up, looking a little put out.

'Don't be upset,' she said. 'It's truly all right. And I liked it. I liked you kissing me... and everything.'

'Perhaps we'd better get you back,' said Peregrine, a little brusquely. He took out a pocket-handkerchief, dabbing his fingers and then his trousers, before throwing it out of the car.

'If you like,' said Ophelia, buttoning her blouse and smoothing down her skirt.

They motored back in silence. Peregrine didn't open the car door for her, didn't help her out, didn't suggest that they might see each other again, and didn't wave farewell.

15

BELOW STAIRS

IT WAS WITH A JAUNTY AIR THAT MCFINN ENTERED THE KITCHEN, helping himself to a doorstop of bread and spreading it thickly with butter.

'You're looking right pleased wi' yerself,' remarked Nessa. She'd been laying fires since five in the morning and was now having a spell with her feet up, drinking tea from one of Cook's special cups and sucking on an oatmeal biscuit.

'Not fer the ears o' young virgins,' he replied. 'Although perhaps there're fewer o' those in this place than we might think.'

'None of yer saucy talk, McFinn,' remonstrated Mrs. Beesby, spooning molasses into the bottom of a bowl destined to hold a treacle pudding. 'All my lassies be good 'uns. You leave them be and they'll stay that way!'

'Absolutely, Mrs. B,' answered McFinn, giving a mock bow. 'I only keep them on their toes. Even virgins need something to think on when they climb in their beds a'night.'

Jennet sidled over to McFinn with a pot of jam, purposefully placing her posterior within squeezing distance.

'That's enough o' that, Jennet,' said Mrs. Beesby. 'Parsnips won't peel themselves. Get yourself busy.'

'I'm not one for gossip o' course,' began McFinn, cutting a second slice from the loaf. 'But a certain miss from London isnae as refined as she looks.'

'Watch your tongue!' retorted Mrs. Beesby. 'If Mr. Haddock hears ye, you'll be out on yer ear!'

'Only speaking as I find, Mrs. B.' He gave a grin. 'Saw Lady O getting into a gentleman's car, bold as brass, and deposited back here with herself all in a state. And why shouldnae she have her fun like the rest. No saints in this house! We're all food for worms in the end. Might as well have a bit o' mischief afore the wrigglers get us.'

'Says you!' remarked Nessa. 'All I seem to do is sweep and clean and deliver enough food for an army...and it's supposed to happen as if by magic. No one wants to think o' my sweat and toil! Chance'd be a fine thing to have a bit o' fun.'

'You be grateful, lass!' warned Mrs. Beesby. 'Better slaving in this house, where you've a decent bed and meals, than skivvying for some skinflint husband on a forsaken croft, popping out bairns year on year.'

She slapped McFinn's hand away from the walnut cake she'd just put on the rack to cool.

'All I'm saying is that those upstairs might act like butter wouldnae melt, but they're nae better nor worse than the likes of us.' McFinn gave Nessa a saucy wink.

Nessa looked pensively at the leaves in the bottom of her cup. 'That French piece is the flighty one. And how old is she? Nearly thirty and no wedding band!' She gave a sniff. 'Playing the field! Just like the men!'

'My lips are sealed...' said McFinn.

16

A SHOCKING ENCOUNTER

THE WEATHER REMAINED FINE AND OPHELIA, BEING DETERMINED NOT to brood on her recent disappointments, took herself for long walks on the hills, Pudding trotting at her side. Launcelot often accompanied her, sketching from various locations, seeking the perfect spot from which to compose his landscape of the castle. The evenings wore on, with only Enid and the Colonel remaining among their guests.

At night, in her bed, Ophelia's thoughts turned with regularity to Hamish. She read the novels of Miss Braddon and Mrs. Gaskell (and occasionally those of Ms. Enid Ellingmore), her imagination transforming the heroes into broad-shouldered figures sporting beards of auburn.

One particular morning when Launcelot had settled in his studio, being ready to prepare his canvas, Ophelia resolved to take a picnic to the loch, wishing to lose herself in the well-leafed copy of *Lady Chatterley's Lover*.

Pudding she had left with her grandmother. Alongside Aphrodite, she would be receiving a bath. Having romped in the bracken before breakfast, both dogs had emerged tangled in burrs, proudly sporting the scent of something unmentionable.

Hamish, the Comte, and Felicité had returned late the night before, and Ophelia had managed, so far, to avoid bumping into them.

By the water where Ophelia spread her blanket, the air was thick with the communal hum of bees and the fragrance of corn marigolds and lady's bedstraw. She kicked off her shoes, removed her stockings, and laid herself out to receive the sun's warmth. No doubt, she'd end up with a grass stain from lolling about, but it was too hot to worry about such things.

About her, insects clicked and rubbed their legs in excited friction. The humidity was such that even the biting midges seemed too oppressed to bother in their labours.

Ophelia bit into an apple and began reading. As she turned the pages, she couldn't help but ponder on how variable satisfaction with the sexual act could be. One minute, Lady Chatterley was thinking how ridiculous it all was, with Mellors' buttocks bouncing towards the finish line, and the next, she was rolling on waves of ecstatic darkness.

Languor settled over Ophelia, not just from the sunshine but from reading Mr. Lawrence's sensuous, rhythmic prose. Her limbs were heavy and yet a restlessness tickled inside her. Velvet-tongued, a voice within was calling to Ophelia. She needed something, or someone.

She was just pondering whether a dip in the loch might soothe her restive state when, sitting up, she caught sight of a male figure in the distance. The man skirted around the side of the castle and looked about, before running to the shadow of the walled garden. He hastily crossed the short distance to the edge of the woods, and disappeared into the trees.

It looked like McFinn, the footman, though she hadn't seen him out of uniform before and couldn't be sure.

How very strange, she thought. *It must be his day off and he's taking a walk, but why is he behaving so furtively? What can he be up to?*

McFinn, like any other man, was entitled to his secrets, Ophelia concluded, but her curiosity was now piqued and her legs were itching to take her somewhere. She slipped on her shoes and walked some way around the edge of the loch before entering the shade of the trees near to where McFinn had done so.

At first, the canopy was open enough to allow beams to filter through, the path moving from light to dark to light again. It was mysterious, and oddly inviting. As she progressed deeper, the woods became sunless and sounds were more muted. She wasn't afraid, though vague shapes fluttered from tree to tree. Fat berries glistened within the brambles and mushroom clusters hung between the knots of trees. The air was full of sap, and moss, and damp.

She stepped carefully, feeling that to make too much noise would be unwise. Somewhere, up ahead, she could hear the cracking of twigs and soft grunts. Did wolves or wild boar still roam such places?

Ophelia heard a sharp, high-pitched cry of anguish and ran forward, wondering if someone was hurt—then stopped to scan the ground, fearful that old-fashioned man-traps might lie hidden, where few ever trod.

The cry grew louder, more insistent, and was punctuated by a female voice.

'Conquer me my little soldier. I must have the piercing of your sword! *Mais oui! Encore! Oui, oui, oui!'*

No more than a dozen steps farther on, Ophelia saw a man's pale backside, and another form, fully naked, bent before him.

The woman's fleshy cheeks received his thrusts.

Ophelia's heart thundered. Fortunately, neither had heard her approach. She crouched, hiding her face in her hands, wishing that she'd never left the comfort of the sun and the amusement of her book. Her limbs had lost all power to move.

Felicité's voice rang through the stillness. *'Mon amoureux! Plongez-moi. Plus fort! Plus fort!'*

Ophelia peeped through her fingers.

McFinn groaned and arched, gripping Felicité's hips fast against his groin.

'Mon Dieu! C'est énorme!' gasped Felicité.

The pair gave full voice to the fulfilment of their pleasures, Felicité bucking beneath McFinn's efforts.

'What a marvellous lover you are, McFinn,' purred Felicité, standing up to brush leaves from her knees. 'I 'ave many, but you are among the best. I am not the porcelain doll. I like to be shaken.'

McFinn gave a low chuckle as Felicité turned, placing her elegant fingers upon his appendage.

'I hope you soon 'ave more for me,' she teased coquettishly.

The last thing Ophelia saw was Felicité dropping to her knees again, closing her mouth around what McFinn proudly offered her.

Legs quivering, Ophelia crept away, still hearing the lovers' groans. She'd been fearful of discovery and shocked by what she'd seen, yet her flesh had responded. She ached with desire; more even than on reading of Lady Chatterley's illicit rendezvous.

She was appalled, not so much at her body's rebellious arousal, as at Felicité's behaviour. What of Hamish? Were they no longer in love?

At the edge of the trees, Ophelia clutched her stomach and expelled the apple and cheese she'd eaten less than an hour ago. The thought of Hamish's anguish sent a stab of pain through her abdomen. He'd be devastated, surely. No decent man deserved this.

It seemed an age since she'd lain on her blanket, wrapped in sunshine. She looked up at the castle.

Hamish was setting deckchairs on the terrace.

Ophelia bundled up her belongings, wishing now to hurry back. As she approached, Hamish was helping Ebenezer to sit, tucking a rug around the old man's knees, crouching to chat with him.

'Sure you're warm enough now? I'll pop in and get you a dram of whisky and that new copy of *Country Life*.'

'You're a good lad, Hamish,' wheezed Ebenezer. 'Make it a large one, of Laphroaig. Or you could bring the bottle.' He gave a grin.

'Steady on! It's only two in the afternoon,' answered Hamish, but he patted his shoulder. 'I'll see what I can do.'

Reaching the terrace steps, Ophelia tried to compose herself, to prevent her voice from quavering as she spoke. 'Isn't it a beautiful day? Good idea to sit out, Ebenezer.'

'Aye,' he replied, amiable for once. 'It's welcome to feel a bit of warmth on the old bones.'

Hamish glanced over his shoulder at her and gave a rueful smile. 'I don't suppose you've seen Felicité, have you? We missed breakfast, took an early bite of lunch, and she said she'd go for a walk but it's not like her to stroll out alone.'

'I have seen her, yes,' Ophelia began. The words were on the tip of her tongue. 'I'm sure she'll be finished soon...I mean, back soon.' She willed her eyes not to roam to the trees.

'Ah...thanks,' said Hamish. 'Stay there. I'll bring out a chair for you.' His animosity seemed to have dissipated. Presumably, he'd had an enjoyable time in Edinburgh.

'Thank you but I won't. I've a slight headache. Too much sun probably...' She wanted so much to sit down with him, to tell him that nothing had happened in the linen cupboard, to make him think well of her again.

Then she remembered what had happened in the motorcar with Peregrine, and how much she'd enjoyed it—at the time. And there was her behaviour with the Comte in the conservatory...

Perhaps she'd be best off staying away from Hamish altogether. Perhaps she was as much of a fly-by-night as Felicité, and whatever was going on between him and her, she shouldn't allow herself to be brought into the midst of it.

At the same time she fought the urge to fling her arms around him, to raise her mouth, and speak only with kisses. Her legs, weak, hesitated, and the moment passed. She turned and walked inside. A great deal remained unsaid.

The evening passed in a haze. The conversation was all of Edinburgh —the shops Felicité had visited, the locket Hamish had bought her, the softness of the beds at the Caledonian Hotel, and the intimacy of the dining arrangements. Ophelia could hardly bear to listen.

All the while, Ophelia looked from Felicité to McFinn, moving about the table with his serving dishes. She wondered if Mr. Lawrence's inspiration for his book had come from something similar —the grand lady hobnobbing with her bit of rough.

Felicité was, as ever, the delightful coquette, her fingers upon Hamish's collar, his cheek, his arm. She listened attentively to the synopsis of Enid's work in progress and offered her opinion. Everyone was enchanted, Ebenezer included.

Meanwhile, McFinn appeared in full command of himself, eyes resting upon the picture rail of the opposite wall, face without expression—the perfect servant. Only when Felicité rose from the table to retire to the drawing room, and winced a little, complaining of some pain in her knee, did Ophelia see the hint of a smirk flicker upon the footman's face.

To Ophelia's surprise, Felicité sought her out on the window seat, as Launcelot joined Morag, Constance and Enid at a hand of Bridge, and Hamish engaged Ebenezer in a game of dominoes. The Comte retreated behind a book.

'Men are curious creatures, are they not?' Felicité began.

'No more than we are,' snapped Ophelia, wishing intently that she might excuse herself. 'We're all more than we seem.'

'I do not say that they are complicated,' Felicité continued. 'Quite the contrary.' She cast a sidelong glance at Hamish. 'Men like to be fed and well-bedded.'

'More than that, surely,' remonstrated Ophelia. 'Like us, they want to feel purposeful.' Her temper was rising. 'They want to be loved too, don't you think? And to trust, and share their life honestly with someone.' A wave of indignation swept over Ophelia. Had Felicité no shame?

'Ha!' Felicité waved her hand dismissively, but kept an amiable expression. 'They like to be flattered and to be charmed. Men also like to feel a little unsafe. Too much reassurance is not a good thing. Keep them on their toes, *non*?'

Hamish looked up from his game and smiled, clearly pleased to see the two of them chatting.

'I don't believe a relationship should be founded on manipulation and secrets.' Ophelia's cheeks were burning. She stood up, wishing to move away, but Felicité caught her wrist.

'You underestimate inventions, *ma chère*. We all make versions of ourselves, do we not? We tip in the salt, or sugar, to please the taste? We present what others wish to see.'

Ophelia shook her hand free and excused herself.

Repulsive woman, Ophelia fumed. And yet, some part of her worried that she was no better. Didn't she, Ophelia, have her own secrets? And more than one face?

Once in her bed, the oblivion of sleep evaded her. First hot, then cold, she tossed. She wondered if she were coming down with summer flu, dozed briefly, then awoke from a terrible dream.

Her face had been pressed with pillows, as if to suffocate her, and she could find no escape. She sat up, gasping for air.

Throwing on her dressing gown, Ophelia went to the window and opened it, letting in the breeze. It was a cool night, and the sky almost clear. A few torn strips of cloud laced the moon. She closed her eyes and concentrated on breathing deeply.

Crows were cawing down in the woods, refusing to settle. They rose as one, swooped over the canopy, then alighted again, flapping and fussing.

Ophelia heard low voices, that of a man and woman. She looked down, to see if anyone were on the terrace. All was quiet. Then, she heard them again.

Leaning farther out, Ophelia noticed a window open to her right along the wall. Voices again, this time louder, as if in argument.

Frowning, Ophelia realized that the window might be that of Felicité's room. She listened. The voices continued—one masculine, insistent. That of the female rose in a sob then fell silent.

A chill passed over Ophelia. She would not act the spy. There had been enough of that for one day. She pulled the latch closed and returned to her bed.

17

A WRIGGLING FISH

WHEN THE EARLY MORNING SUN RAISES MIST OVER LOCHS AND RIVERS, fishermen find their tackle quivering in anticipation.

Hamish was no exception. He woke with the dawn, his mind already on his rods, lines, and reels. He turned to the blonde head upon his pillow, and offered a proposal to which he already knew the answer.

Would a certain Parisienne mademoiselle join him in sitting patiently, and quietly, for an hour or two in hope of netting a good catch? The lady in question turned her lips to his for a sleepy kiss, and returned to her slumbers.

Emerging upon the terrace, it was with surprise that he found Ophelia sitting upon a deckchair in her dressing gown, her eyes seemingly focused on the far distance yet looking very much as if her thoughts were focused inwards.

She gave him a smile, though a weak one. The shadows beneath her eyes bore witness to a troubled night.

Ophelia took in Hamish's fishing tweeds, waterproofs and the full complement of his equipment. 'Bit early, isn't it?'

'Ordinarily, yes'—he admitted—'but with the weather so fine, it's the best part of the day. The trout'll be hiding later. They'll be near the surface just now, feeding on their fill of insects.'

'Poor, helpless things,' sighed Ophelia. 'Having a lovely feast one minute and then thrashing in your net the next.'

'You weren't complaining when they were on your plate,' he pointed out.

'We women are full of contradictions, aren't we,' said Ophelia. 'But you're right of course.'

Stirred by a sudden impulse, she announced, 'I should come with you! I want to come with you, I mean. It's just where I'd like to be, on the loch. You don't mind, do you?'

'As delightful as that would be, you're hardly dressed for it. And I'd rather not wait…don't mean to be rude…'

'Absolutely,' answered Ophelia, standing up. 'Not to worry; I'll come just as I am. There's no one here to see, or be bothered. It'll be at least another two hours before anyone upstairs is stirring. I left Pudding snoring. And I've come down in my brogues, not my slippers, so it'll be all right.'

'You're going to fish in your dressing gown?'

'Why not?' said Ophelia. 'It's a perfectly sturdy dressing gown; quite warm enough!'

Hamish eyed the woollen robe, fastened at the front by a tasselled rope. 'Right, well, off we go then! We can borrow another rod from the groundsmen's shed on the way. Take the knapsack for me if you like— there's a thermos of coffee and some rolls in there. We can breakfast while we wait for the trout to bite.'

Ophelia had been in a wooden dinghy before, rowed on the Serpentine in Hyde Park. This really wasn't much different, except that she hadn't been surrounded by the grandeur of a Scottish glen on the last occasion. Nor had she been seated across from a man to whom she was most certainly attracted. She watched him take the oars, pulling them back with a repeated roll of his shoulders, extending and pulling again.

'There's no need to go far. Fish'll mostly be in the shallower margins of the loch, where the water's a good temperature. They'll swim farther in, where it's deeper, and cooler, as the morning wears on,' explained Hamish.

If, a mere month ago, someone had told Ophelia that she would be discovering how to tie a fly (one of Hamish's own making, of fur and feather), and how to cast her line in just the right way, to imitate the movement of an insect upon the surface of the water, she would have spluttered in scorn.

'That's it,' said Hamish, as Ophelia managed a fair example of an arbor knot. 'We'll try a non-slip loop next. It gives more flexibility for the fly, so it bobs and shakes in the water, like the real thing. You'll soon have the trout fooled and be reeling them in.'

'Perhaps this isn't so different from debutante life,' she laughed. 'Fooling the waiting fish with a bit of artifice, catching them on a hook and landing them in the bag. My mother might be proud of me yet!'

'Isn't she already?' asked Hamish. 'I'm sure she must be. You're no fool. You know your worth, I think. It takes some people a long time to learn that.'

Ophelia allowed herself the pleasure of the compliment. She surveyed him, and Hamish perused her in turn. He seemed in no hurry to look away.

'It would be nice to think so,' she said at last.

'Time to cast,' declared Hamish. 'The scent from your hands will have transferred to the lure, which may deter the fish from biting, but we'll see...I should have gotten you to rub your hands in the dirt first.'

'That I may have objected to,' admitted Ophelia. 'We'll find out if they're partial to a dash of Shalimar.'

Ophelia sat, Hamish close behind her, guiding her in casting back the reel and allowing her line to flick out upon the water, landing her fly not far from the boat, where she might watch it, and see when the trout took the lure.

'That's it, well done,' said Hamish, his hand upon her wrist, working in parallel to her. She could feel the warmth of his chest at her back and the strength of his arm against her own. She became aware, as she had not before, of wearing nothing but her nightdress against her skin. A prickle of sensation rippled through her.

'We'll let the boat drift broadside to the wind. You cast downwind, and we'll see how we go. Just avoid standing up. We don't want you toppling in. I'm not explaining to Morag why I've got you out here in your nightclothes.'

Ophelia didn't trust her voice not to waiver, or for a gush of words not to emerge, telling Hamish what she believed better to conceal. She was afraid even to turn her face towards him. He would surely see her feelings for him, her desire.

If he reached to untie her dressing gown, to slip his hands about her waist, she would let him. Her mouth, and her body, would be his.

So lost was she in this reverie that she almost forgot where she was and what she was supposedly intent upon. It was the excitement in Hamish's voice that returned her to the moment.

'First bite!'

'Oh look, look.' Ophelia's voice rose in similar joyful expectation.

'Shhhh, not so loud!' Hamish warned her. 'Don't want to frighten the rest away. Gently now, turn the handle on the reel, and bring it in.'

'It's pulling quite hard. Oh, poor thing. It's swimming for its life. It's struggling.'

'Keep steady. You can do it,' assured Hamish. 'That's it, keep going.'

A perfect spotted trout emerged, gasping, from the water.

'Oh, it's beautiful!' declared Ophelia. 'Such colours— all the greens and browns of the glen, and so white on its belly.'

The fish, being not yet willing to utter its last breath, gave a mighty thrash; Ophelia swung the line to one side and slapped the trout against the side of Hamish's head.

'Oh, I am sorry!' said Ophelia, and, without thinking, stood up, the fish flapping wildly in the air. She reached to unhook its mouth, and the trout flipped abruptly from her fingers. With an indignant swish of fin, it leapt back to its watery domain.

'Steady there,' warned Hamish, grabbing her ankle, but it was too late.

Ophelia found her centre of gravity no longer planted firmly in the boat but sailing through the air, sending her for a chill morning dip.

Under the circumstances, it was unsurprising that she gave a screech and dropped the fishing rod. She was submerged only for a moment—long enough to see the trout whisk away. Spitting water, Ophelia popped up, her dressing gown billowing around her as she kicked her feet in their heavy brogues. Pondweed stroked her calves.

No more than a handful of strokes brought her to the edge of the dinghy, from where Hamish looked over the side. Despite wet tendrils of hair across her eyes, she could see that he was more amused than irritated.

His arm reached under hers and hauled her in. Curls dripping around her face, she scrabbled to right herself, desperate to regain her dignity. She was like a bedraggled cat pulled from a barrel. Her sopping clothes were already making a significant puddle in the boat. And she'd lost a shoe.

'Just sit there. Don't move. Don't touch anything.' Hamish told her, clearly having trouble in keeping from laughing.

He took off his jacket and placed it about her shoulders.

'Damn trout!' retorted Ophelia, refusing to look at him. 'You could have warned me!'

'You had a wriggler there, right enough.' Hamish began pulling on the oars, taking them back.

'I'm utterly wet!' said Ophelia.

'Mmmm-hmmm.'

'And I'm cold.'

'I imagine you are.' Hamish conceded.

'I don't think I like fishing after all.' Ophelia coughed up a little water.

'Open the flask of coffee,' suggested Hamish. 'It'll make you feel better.'

It did.

Having had several sips, she offered the cup to Hamish.

'Sorry about losing the other rod.'

'It was an old one. Not to worry.' He gave a smile. 'You were doing so well. Shouldn't let this put you off.'

'I was enjoying it...until that silly fish starting flapping.' Ophelia pulled Hamish's jacket closer. It smelt of peat and pine-sap.

'It only wanted its freedom I suppose,' she added. 'I'd struggle too if I were on the end of a hook.'

It occurred to her that this was just what she'd been doing for a long time, in London—wriggling to extricate herself.

They reached the landing stage, where Hamish tied the boat and helped her out. She stood for a moment, reluctant to move, though knowing that she should change before she caught a chill.

Hamish, standing tall above her, placed his hands on her shoulders. 'We're none of us perfect, you know. We're all seeking our way. Sometimes, we don't realize what makes us happy until it's no longer on offer. Best to grasp happiness where you find it.'

He looked out over the water. 'I taught my wife to fish here, on this loch. It was a long time ago, but I haven't forgotten.'

A lump sat in Ophelia's throat, refusing to budge.

Damn Felicité. What's she playing at? she thought. *Isn't he enough? He deserves contentment. He deserves love.*

Half a minute passed, then another. Hamish's hands rested still upon her shoulders. Neither of them spoke. Ophelia was sure that he'd kiss her. She wanted him to.

At last, breaking the spell, Hamish said, 'It's close on seven o'clock. Easier if no one spots you traipsing mermaid-like through the house. I'll drop in the kitchen and send Maggie to mop behind you.'

Ophelia took off her shoe to run barefoot over the grass.

18

STORMFIRE

ANOTHER DAY PASSED IN MINOR AMUSEMENTS AND REFLECTIONS ON the weather, until they gathered for dinner. Felicité appearing in a pale peach gown, the delicate silk hugging her slender body, leaving her naked to the waist at the back. Glass beads adorned the hem and the centre plunge of the neckline.

Ophelia found herself looking from Felicité to McFinn—as he served the vegetables to each course, as he cleared plates, and replenished their water glasses. If glances there were, they were undeniably discreet. Ophelia doubted the others were aware of anything untoward. However, Hamish appeared distracted, eating little and failing to keep the thread of conversations.

It was a relief to Ophelia to go to bed, although she tossed beneath the covers. Pudding grunted in complaint, finding no difficulty in her own slumbers. She stretched, paws kneading Ophelia's arm, before lying still.

As she often did, Ophelia rose to go to the window. The moon was dazzlingly bright. Opening the latch to let in the night air, Ophelia closed her eyes. She was back in the wooden boat, with Hamish. Her fingers untied the ribbon of her dressing gown, letting it fall open. She knelt forward, reaching for him, pressing to his chest. His mouth closed upon hers in a kiss.

Ophelia heard voices as she had the night before. They were certainly arguing. Leaning out, Ophelia saw again the window open to her right. She heard a sharp slap, and a returning cry of alarm.

Frowning, Ophelia pulled the uppermost blanket from her bed and wrapped it about her shoulders, her dressing gown being still laundered. She closed her door quietly behind her. All was dark, and still, with a chill draft wafting down the corridor. She wrapped the blanket tighter.

Placing her hand along the wall to feel her way, Ophelia tiptoed forward, past the large bathroom and the water closet, stopping at the third door. The voices within were muffled by the heavy wood but she recognized Felicité's feminine lilt and the deeper voice of the Comte. The two spoke in rapid French, making it impossible for Ophelia to understand.

In the Great Hall, the clock chimed two.

Again, Ophelia heard a slap and, this time, Felicité swearing.

No matter her feelings towards the Frenchwoman, Ophelia was adamant that no one should endure physical abuse. It was 1928, and women needed to stick together.

Some families were more patriarchal than others and the Comte, she imagined, was not one to cross. Had he discovered Felicité's liaison with the footman and chosen to punish her? It seemed barbaric, although women had been sent to asylums for less, in the days of her grandmother's youth.

Kneeling, Ophelia placed her eye to the keyhole. Heart racing, her breath came in ragged bursts. It struck her that, were someone to appear in the corridor, her spying would place her in a poor light. And yet…she needed to see more before she intervened.

Felicité was bent over the end of her bed, her nightgown raised. Ophelia watched as the Comte gave his step-sister's bare bottom a vicious pinch, followed by a smack from his open palm. It caught her on the underside of her right cheek. Ophelia heard Felicité whimper and imagined the sharp sting of it.

She swore again, '*Arrêtez! Monstre!*'

The Comte delivered three further blows in quick succession. Felicité cried out, but the shriek died in her throat, turning to a soft moan.

Ophelia was steeling herself to turn the handle of the door, whatever unpleasantness it brought upon her head, when she saw the Comte press his hand between Felicité's legs.

This time, rather than protesting, Ophelia heard Felicité groan, unmistakably, in pleasure, and urge on her tormentor.

'*Vite! Tu es diabolique! Je ne peux pas attendre.*'

Ophelia's breath became shorter as she watched, seeing the Comte's thumb nestle within the woman's fur. He drew it back and forth with measured relish.

She should turn away and forget what she'd seen. The Comte and Felicité weren't blood relatives. They were flouting no laws except those of common decency; Hamish, surely, could have no idea.

Ophelia placed her hand over the keyhole. She must return to her room.

Ophelia reproached herself for having not once, but twice, invaded the privacy of others. Moreover, she was torn utterly in how to behave towards the Comte, Felicité, and Hamish, not to mention McFinn.

She couldn't stop thinking of what she'd seen. Hamish, it appeared, knew nothing of Felicité's actions. If he did, he was more liberal than she'd imagined.

Noticing her agitation, Morag suggested that Ophelia take out one of the horses, and she agreed readily.

She was inspecting them to see which might best suit her, when she heard footsteps in the tack room and turned to see Hamish. A flush bloomed through her body.

'Heard you were riding. Don't mind if I join you? Here, take Esmeralda. She's quietest,' he offered.

'That's very kind,' Ophelia conceded as Hamish helped Lyle, the stable lad, saddle up the mare. Ophelia watched as Hamish whispered into the horse's ear, stroking her neck. Esmeralda was, evidently, enchanted. She reached to nibble his sleeve as he placed the bit in her mouth.

'Take it easy,' warned Hamish, leading the horse out for her, 'Esmeralda's a good filly but she'll take her head if you give her the chance.'

Ophelia suppressed a twinge of annoyance. She'd had enough of being told what to do under her mother's eye. Moreover, Hamish's proximity was sending her knees a-quiver. It was a pathetic state of affairs, and it was below her dignity to let him see the effect he was having on her.

I must take myself in hand.

'You needn't be so patronizing. I've been riding since I was four! I know how to handle a horse.'

Wishing to hide her trembling lip, she set off at a gallop, heading towards the dense forest west of the loch. Hamish, barely having had time to saddle his own ride, vaulted on. Standing high in the stirrups, he called out to her. 'Slow down, you fool!'

Ophelia, however, heard not a word, the wind having picked up. It came blowing down from the mountains, whisking away all good sense. She spurred Esmeralda on, entering beneath the whipping branches.

As she rounded the second bend in the path, they came upon a stag, antlers lowered. Esmeralda, panicked, made an ill-timed leap to the side, to avoid being pierced by the deer's horns. Ophelia clung on desperately as the horse twisted in mid-air but found herself unseated, and thrown.

The stag darted away, leaving Ophelia, dazed, reclining in a puddle of mud. It had taken some of the impact of her fall but she was sodden, and the stuffing had been knocked from her.

'Well, I don't suppose you'll do that again in a hurry,' said Hamish, appearing through the trees and surveying the situation.

She was lying in filth, slime oozing up between her legs. Ophelia winced, attempting to sit up. Her ankle was throbbing and her head spinning somewhat.

Hamish slid down from his horse, kneeling at her side. Seeing she was in pain, he became more solicitous.

'We'll get you up and sort you out. You've had a shock.' He lifted her, one arm under her knees and the other across her back.

She hadn't been carried since she was a child, taken up the stairs by her father. Even in her muddled state, she thought how nice it was, but how dark it had become. Menacing clouds were flowing over the crags, bringing fat raindrops, rustling the leaves above them.

With the first flash of brilliance splitting the sky, Hamish's stallion let out a snort of fear. As a deep, monstrous rumble travelled across the canyon of the glen, the two horses decided that enough was enough and bolted clear.

'Damnation!'

'What's the matter, Hamish,' mumbled Ophelia. 'Do you want to kiss me? You can if you like. You're a very good kisser...' Her eyes closed and her body went limp in his arms.

Another lightning tongue lashed the peaks, followed closely by thunder. The storm was coming closer.

She awoke upon a cottage sofa, to the sweet smell of burning wood. Hamish was crouched before the stove, feeding it logs from a basket.

Her velvet coat had been draped over a chair to dry. Rain beat heavily upon the window.

'I'm cold,' she said, making him look up.

He'd taken off her boots, though not her socks. They hung limply from her feet, sodden and misshapen.

'It's because I'm wet through,' she went on, and she was, every bit of her. The storm had finished what the puddle had begun. She seemed to be spending more time than she'd like in damp clothing.

'You're awake then. That's good. Your ankle feels like it's swelling.

Try to keep it raised.' From a cupboard, Hamish brought out an old shirt and two blankets.

Ophelia shrugged off her jacket, leaving it in a heap on the floor.

'Don't look.' She pulled at the buttons of her blouse, then yanked it over her head and wriggled out of her jodhpurs and underthings, trying not to mind the discomfort as she moved.

No bruises were showing yet, but she was tender all over.

The shirt he'd given her was too rough to button closely, so she left the upper fasteners loose. The blankets she tucked round her legs, and leant back again into the cushions of the sofa.

'Good that you're talking again.' Hamish lifted down a bottle and poured some of the liquid into a tin cup. 'Drink this. It'll warm you.'

'Where's Esmeralda?' Ophelia frowned. She remembered partly what had happened.

'Both bolted, but they'll find their way back, don't worry.' He took his handkerchief and dabbed a corner in the whisky, using it to wipe a streak of mud from her cheek. 'I couldn't carry you far.'

'This is your cabin, isn't it?' she said, rather obviously. Propped against the wall were variously-sized axes and other tools.

A bright flash lit the gloom, followed by a low growl, as of a subterranean monster waking in its lair. The door shook.

'What's out there?' she whimpered.

'Nothing. It's just the wind.'

'They're rattling the door. Don't let them in!' Ophelia pulled a blanket higher.

'I think you've bumped your head, as well as that ankle,' said Hamish.

He sat beside her on the little sofa and moved her legs across his lap, so that her foot was elevated. He held the cup as she took a sip.

'It's turning me warm inside.' The fiery whisky numbed her lips, making them tingle. 'It's the same feeling I have when I'm with you.'

He looked at her for a moment then smiled. 'You won't remember any of this in the morning.'

The wind rattled the door again, in savage spite, and she jumped.

'Do you think of her? Your wife?' she asked abruptly. She wouldn't have dared broach the subject before, but all sorts of things seemed to be tumbling out.

Hamish stared at her in surprise then shrugged wearily.

The wind blew down the chimney, making the woodstove flare.

At last, he said, 'Yes, I do… often.'

Ophelia thought of the baby but said nothing. Instead, she listened to Hamish breathing, looking at his profile as he gazed at the fire.

'Sometimes, it's as if I'm on a bridge and can't see the other side. Not sure where I'm going. Can't go back and too afraid to move forward.' He paused. 'Plenty of warm beds on offer, and I've had my share, but I'd rather there be love between the sheets.'

Ophelia found herself looking into his eyes, green-flecked and framed with thick, darkly ginger lashes.

'It's hard to know if the other person feels the same way,' he continued. 'I wonder if we just love what we imagine them to be.'

His mouth, which she had seen angry and admonishing, jesting and playful, was soft now.

'They all think I should marry again—become a husband, have children.'

'What is it that you see in her?' asked Ophelia.

'Felicité?' Hamish rubbed the back of his neck. 'She's attractive of course, and vivacious, but it's more than that. She doesn't hide her nature, or make apologies for it. She says and does as she likes. It's refreshing.' Hamish spoke softly. 'I don't want to be alone.'

Ophelia saw the sadness in his face, and the tiredness, but also the resilience. Placing her hand on his arm, she said, 'Neither do I.'

The storm and failing daylight had made the room darker. Lit only by the stove, the shadows were thick. Tremors continued to shake the roof and windows of the cabin.

'I don't think you know what you want.' Hamish sighed. 'When you do, you'll be happier.' His gaze stroked her skin, dark and searching.

She wasn't thinking as she fumbled with the buttons at the front of her shirt. Some moments aren't for thinking. She opened them one by one. The glow from the stove lit the curves of her body. Taking his hand, she found it more calloused than she'd expected. Tentatively, she brought it to her breast, pressing his roughened skin to her softness. She wasn't greatly endowed, her bosom fitting neatly into his cupping palm.

He must feel my heart, and the way it's racing.

He sat very still, as if to touch her further would break the enchantment. She was all but naked, light and dark dancing across her body.

I should be blushing. I should turn away.

But she didn't.

He leaned forward, lips parted, and there was nothing in her but the melting desire to return the force of his mouth, to be wrapped tight in his arms, to feel the strength of him. Drinking deeply, his kiss held both torment and need.

And then his longing overcame him. His mouth was at her breast, his beard scraping her nipple.

Ophelia was lost to sensation, laying back as he kissed and licked and suckled.

Moving lower, he pushed aside the blankets and grazed her belly. His hands were under her hips, raising her sex to meet his mouth. The shock of his tongue made her gasp, stroking her, curling to the nub of her sex, making her twist in agonized joy.

Wanting more, she writhed, knowing there was more, and that, of all men, it was Hamish she wanted to share this moment with her.

To show her what it was for a man and woman to love one another physically.

To show her what she'd conjured many times in her imagination.

Fleetingly, she remembered the Comte, who'd devoured her with his mouth in the same way little more than a week before.

But not the same!

With a handful of Hamish's hair in her fist, she whimpered.

When he raised his head, his eyes were darkly dilated. There was desire, but not the conquering kind which delights in possession and control.

Hamish's expression was both searching and tender—as if his quest was only to secure her happiness.

Quickly, he threw off his shirt and trousers, and she drank in the beauty of his body.

So muscular, darkened from the sun upon his back. His arms were strong, and his stomach hard and flat. And the part of him she craved to take inside her was most beautiful of all, standing proud from the auburn thatch of hair about his groin.

'I'm not afraid,' she said.

There was nothing brutish, clumsy, or awkward as he lowered his body into her softness. Wordless, she allowed herself to be enfolded in pleasure, while the storm raged around them.

19

THE COLD LIGHT OF DAY

SHE WOKE TO GREY EARLY LIGHT AND CHILL, THE FIRE HAVING GONE out. The storm's howling had passed and it was quiet, as if all nature had ceased breathing.

Ophelia was thirsty and muddle-headed, her limbs languorously limp, heavy with memories. Sitting up, looking expectantly for Hamish, her ankle ached and another part of her too.

Hamish had been gentle and she'd been so eager that there had been no pain--as she'd been led to believe there might be. Rather, there was fleeting discomfort, shock at finding her body able to accommodate him—then a strange, compelling need to have him move inside her.

Only at the end had he thrust in a determined, relentless way that seemed for his own satisfaction, raising her knee and entering more deeply. Even then, she'd wanted him to keep going—for each long stroke made her burn, needing him more than ever.

She'd clasped him all the tighter, sensing that this was the moment they were closest of all, with Hamish's arousal buried in her. And suddenly she'd been overcome with the desire to laugh and cry all at once, as a shaking, throbbing sensation had taken hold of her—not just in that place where they were joined, but travelling through all her body and back again to burst in sparks and flames.

Oh, she didn't know how to describe it—but it had been the most wonderful thing.

Hamish must have thought so too for, as her insides rippled and shivered, he'd let out an unexpected, tormented groan and had gone quite rigid, a look of surprise in his eyes. She'd felt the same pulsing from his body that she'd felt in her own, and it had made her squeak, for he'd touched her even more deeply than before.

But it was all heavenly, and she'd been suffused with the most blazing happiness when he relaxed at last, resting between her thighs, with his head upon her breast.

The most embarrassing thing was how wet everything had become, but Hamish had been an angel, damping his shirt for her so that she might wash a little.

And then they had lain down together on the sofa, with Hamish embracing her from behind, pulling her close so that she was entirely warm—and had gotten to sleep almost immediately.

But where was he now?

Softly, as if afraid of whom she might summon, she called out for him.

There was no reply.

From outside, she heard the crack of splitting wood. She eased herself up, wincing, and hobbled into the morning air, the old shirt pulled over her head and a blanket wrapped close about her.

Hamish let his axe swing a full arc into the waiting log, tossing kindling to one side. Ophelia leaned against the door, watching the strength of his shoulders.

How much can change in a single day.

Never before had her heart fluttered like this. Breathing now required concentration. It was happiness, she realized—an overwhelming joy.

He stooped to pick up the wood and turned, seeing her. He smiled, but without the warmth she'd been expecting. 'Go back in. You need to keep that foot up.'

Searching his face, a chasm opened in her chest, dark and cold. 'Hamish?' she prompted, feeling her voice quiver.

'I'll chop more wood, and then head up to the house to collect the horses. Clearly, you can't walk on that ankle.'

'Last night...' she began, but words failed her.

Hamish took up the axe again, steadfastly avoiding her eye.

What had happened between them had been wondrous. She refused to believe that he couldn't feel the same way—but it was too humiliating to entreat him to explain.

Had he been disappointed? By her lack of experience or finesse? It had been her first time, after all; he knew that, surely. She would get better at it. And, if there was something he wanted her to do, that she didn't know about yet, he could show her. She would do anything he asked.

Hugging herself, Ophelia returned to the cabin, curling up on the sofa, turning her head towards the cushions to hide her welling tears.

He'd made no promises or declarations, yet she'd been convinced their lovemaking meant something.

Of course, there was Felicité.

But she didn't love Hamish—not really! Ophelia was convinced. If she hadn't been, she would never have let Hamish kiss her, let alone any of the rest.

She had some moral compass, and stealing a man from under the nose of another woman wasn't her style; except that, in a way, she'd done just that.

Although it was hardly fair for her to take all the blame.

Hamish hadn't let his entanglement with the Frenchwoman deter him from giving Ophelia a damn good bedding—and he'd been so affectionate and considerate afterwards. Only the cold light of day had changed his mind, so it seemed.

Ophelia's tears ebbed, replaced by anger, then numb regret.

I should never have let it happen; not with a man already involved elsewhere.

She'd sat in front of him near naked, for goodness sake; had taken his hand and pressed it to her bare breast.

The invitation had been unmistakable.

She'd acted the vamp and gotten just what she was after, without thought for who she might be hurting.

No doubt that was why Hamish was offhand with her. The passions of the night had been replaced with disgust—for the way Ophelia had thrown herself at him. Self-loathing too, perhaps—for he could hardly be feeling good about any of it.

She knew him well enough to surmise that.

Ophelia rubbed away her tears upon the sleeve of the shirt and looked about for her riding clothes.

Hamish had hung them up and they were nearly dry.

She'd just fastened the last buttons of her jacket when the sound of Hamish splitting wood ended, and she heard him climbing the steps beyond the door.

He looked at her briefly—taking in that she'd dressed herself—before kneeling to lay the fire. Within a few minutes, it was blazing again.

'I'll be as quick as I can. Keep the fire going, but stay off the ankle otherwise.' He was business-like in his instructions.

Ophelia couldn't help herself. She looked at him yearningly.

Say something, please! Just a word. Show me that you feel as I do.

But his remorse was clearly stronger than any affection he might harbour. And she had her dignity; she wouldn't beg him for what he wasn't prepared to give freely.

Alone, she sat watching the flames.

It was some time before she heard footsteps on the track. She shuffled out. Hamish had brought Lyle with him.

'Oh, Miss Ophelia,' he puffed, running ahead. 'Mr. Munro says ye turned yer ankle and spent the night here in the bothy. Come on, m'lady, put yer arm over ma shoulder and I'll help ye onto Rosie. She's a steady beast. Ye shall come to nae harm.'

Hamish avoided touching her, letting Lyle take most of her weight, helping only to steady the mare as Ophelia pushed her good foot into the stirrup. He'd fitted a side-saddle, so that she might sit more comfortably, but the awkwardness of it still had her wincing.

Lyle walked alongside her horse, holding the reins while Hamish went on. They made their way slowly, tree branches having come down, making the going difficult. It was little more than two miles to return, but the uneven path jolted her repeatedly.

It was impossible for her to speak to Hamish with Lyle there. No doubt, that was why he'd brought him.

To compose herself, she focused on the stream filled to brimming, rippling over stones and roots, and then the loch, running high upon its banks. Her eyes, however, kept straying to Hamish's back turned adamantly against her. The air, cool and clean, was like breathing cold water, rushing in, raw and ragged.

At last, arriving at the castle, Lyle helped her down. Indecorously, Ophelia was obliged to slide off the saddle into his arms; he was stronger than she expected.

'I'll take over from here,' Hamish told him curtly, leaving Lyle to lead the horses away. He offered her his arm stiffly.

'My dear! Oh! How worried we were!' exclaimed Morag, appearing on the steps, rushing forward to hug Ophelia. 'That terrible storm!'

She took Ophelia's other arm.

'Lyle said he saw you both ride out yesterday, only minutes before the clouds started gathering. Constance assured me that Hamish would look after you both, and she guessed of course that he'd take you to the cabin if there was any trouble.'

Ophelia smiled wanly. Morag's warmth brought a lump to her throat. How lovely it was to have someone saying kind things to her, although she feared it would make her cry.

Constance appeared then, full of solicitous concern.

'Your poor ankle! And you must be ravenous, my dear, not having eaten since yesterday luncheon. Hamish, would you tell cook to bring up some venison stew to Ophelia's room, with plenty of thickly buttered bread, and a pot of tea.'

Hamish nodded his assent and departed, leaving her in the care of the two dowagers.

'Let's get you upstairs and into the bath first,' said Morag. 'Then we'll tuck you into bed.'

They took her, step by step, most carefully. Being undressed as the water ran, Ophelia felt quite four years old again.

'We'll be back in a few minutes, dear,' Constance said, once they'd helped her into the tub. 'Just call if you need us.'

Feeling most dreadfully tired, Ophelia closed her eyes and eased her shoulders under the water. No matter that it was rather brown, having been drawn from the loch. The warmth offered some comfort.

She'd surrendered to Hamish, and he had surrendered to her. A light had flared brightly within her and had been just as abruptly extinguished.

With a new thought crossing her mind, her eyes flew open.

Last night, in the throes of desire, her own and his, they had taken no precautions.

She bit her lip.

2 O

TIME TO THINK

THE DOCTOR CAME AND PRONOUNCED THE ANKLE MERELY SPRAINED. He bandaged it and noted that Ophelia would be fine within a week. She should try her weight on it as soon as she was able. Her ankle continued to ache but the pain of it was nothing compared to the anguish she directed at herself.

She spent the next few days in bed, visited regularly by the two elderly ladies, bringing her treats to tempt her appetite.

At first, she reclined, listless, gazing vaguely out of the window, her thoughts never far from her fear that she might be carrying a new life inside her. She picked up books repeatedly but without the will to read. There was only one visitor her heart pined for, and he failed to come.

It's true what they say. Falling in love is a kind of madness. I was in a delightful dream and now I've woken up.

Ophelia endured the time as best as she could, cursing and crying, then retreating into silence. She slept a great deal, letting healing darkness wrap around her like a cloak.

Her nails were bitten almost to the quick with anxiety, but she was adamant that, if she were "in pig", she'd bring up the baby herself.

Morag would help her. Ophelia might be banished from Polite Society forever more, but what did she care.

As for Hamish, Ophelia had no idea how he'd feel about it. Might he whisk her off to be married? Or never look at her again?

Left to simmer, Ophelia's sense of shock and sadness began to turn to indignation. She'd offered her deepest self and it had been thrown back in her face.

Just wait until I'm on my feet again. I'll have words for Hamish that certainly won't be from any book of etiquette. I'll show him that his regard, or affection, or whatever it is I was hoping for (Ophelia declined to admit the details) *isn't of the slightest consequence!*

Of course, in coming to this conclusion, she wished intently that Hamish would enter and have eyes only for her. He'd beg her forgiveness, which she'd refuse—at least for some minutes—before sinking utterly into his embrace.

Ophelia, in the tedium of those days, became aware of the rhythms of the house more than she ever had when she'd been free to roam. She'd learnt the routines of the housemaids—clearing the ash from the previous night's fire and laying anew; dusting, polishing, changing bed linen, cleaning windows, taking away soiled clothing, and returning it pressed and immaculate. She watched sheepishly as activity took place about her—Nessa and Maggie moving efficiently, eyes cast down, fingers nimble, while their feet softly carried them from one task to the next.

It was with humility and slight embarrassment that she accepted tray after tray, from her breakfast of grapefruit and kipper through to her bedtime cocoa. She was aware that she must be creating extra work. There were endless pots of tea, accompanied by some little confection from Mrs. Beesby, as well as lunch and supper of course.

The maids even took out Pudding on her behalf.

Feeling cold late one night, she considered tugging the bell for an extra hot water bottle. Not long ago, she'd have done so without a second thought for who would be summoned from their bed. Now, she stayed her hand on the rope and withdrew it back under the covers.

Ophelia's days began to merge, one into the next, in lazy, languorous tedium—reading, hobbling to the window, picking at meals.

Meanwhile, the same faces came to visit, telling the same stories and sharing their own version of the same gossip.

Launcelot proved a particularly lively companion, imitating the quarrelsome voice of Ebenezer, the lecherous overtures of the Colonel, and the catty judgements of the Comte and Felicité.

'Ebenezer's in the worst mood imaginable, driving us all mad,' confided Launcelot, passing Ophelia a lemon sherbet. 'We're denounced at least three times daily as servants of the carnal apocalypse!' He rolled his eyes. 'Cook made two pink blancmanges for the table, each topped with a handful of berries; you'd think she'd stripped off and laid herself out for our delectation, such were Ebenezer's comments.' Launcelot gave a mock bow. 'The devil's carriage awaits us if you'd like to put on your slippers.'

Ophelia couldn't help but smile ruefully. 'Poor old thing; he suffers with unmentionable ailments, you know. Piles are no laughing matter.'

'Have you heard about Haddock's harem?' continued Launcelot.

Nearly choking on her tea, Ophelia shook her head.

'Morag asked our gorgeous Hamish to build a smart little coop for the hens, in the hope that this bijou accommodation would inspire them to lay. She thought that the male touch would be the deciding factor.'

Ophelia smarted at the mention of Hamish's name, but nodded her encouragement for Launcelot to continue.

'Haddock, as you know, prides himself on being the most excellent of servants. Her ladyship's whim is his to obey.' Launcelot wiggled his eyebrows suggestively. 'She's made him suitor to her new batch of hens, sent over from Inverness: Faverolles, Frizzles, and Dorkings. He is instructed to stroke from hackle to saddle every evening, tucking them into bed with a tickle under their wattle.'

Ophelia couldn't help but laugh as Launcelot acted out the scenario. It was good to be diverted and forget her broken heart for a while.

'Similarly, he rouses the hens at dawn, greeting each with a kiss upon its comb. He's rewarded not only with their contented trills and peeps but with the finest daily clutch of eggs.'

'I do believe you're making this up!' declared Ophelia. 'I'm not listening to any more of it! You shouldn't make fun of Granny; nor of Haddock.'

'You're right of course. Consider me chastised.'

Ophelia gave him a smack upon the wrist.

Loretta brought her a pile of American *Starlet* magazines and rouged her like Clara Bow, insisting that she had just the right shape of lip to carry off a vermillion shade, and that her eyes were made for kohl and false lashes.

'Good Heavens!' declared Ophelia when Loretta at last permitted her a peek in the dressing table mirror. She tucked her chin into her shoulder and imitated the 'come hither' look so popular in the magazines then stretched her neck, presenting her profile.

'Isn't it marvellous, honey. You're a dead ringer. Ranulph's still keen to sign you up. Everyone wants a piece of Clara; there's not enough to go around.'

Loretta stood behind her, coaxing Ophelia's curls to frame her cheekbones.

I doubt Ranulph will be as keen on seeing me on the silver screen with a huge baby bump, thought Ophelia.

'It's really kind, and this is more fun than I've had in a while, but I don't think so, Loretta.'

Fluttering her false lashes one more time, Ophelia poked her tongue out at her own reflection and sighed. 'It's just not me. I'm really not bothered about being the centre of attention. Having other people look at you all day must be exhausting.'

'Don't you worry, sweetie. I'll tell Ranulph you're a "no". I think he's been sniffing around that French piece. Maybe she fancies being a movie star...'

'It might suit her very well,' admitted Ophelia.

It was on her fifth day of seclusion, soon after Maggie had collected her breakfast tray, that the Comte entered Ophelia's room.

He scattered a selection of French pornographic novels upon the coverlet. 'If you're too distracted to read, you may enjoy the illustrations.'

He gave her a lascivious grin. 'Or you may care to peruse the real thing...' In the twinkling of an eye, he presented his semi-erect member for her appraisal.

Really! Even my own bedroom isn't a safe haven! Ophelia ground her teeth.

'You're right, Comte, I'm far too restless to read. I have something more amusing in mind.' Ophelia smiled as sweetly as she was able. 'Now, place yourself in my hands, and close your eyes.'

Within arm's reach was her bedside cabinet, and in the top drawer, a jar of Benedict's Balsam—that powerful menthol salve known to relieve congested chests and sore muscles. This miracle ointment promised the alleviation of all manner of ailments.

Ophelia took a generous handful and cupped the Comte's quivering appendage, slathering the unguent liberally down the length.

'*Mon Dieu!*' He jumped up, spitting oaths beyond Ophelia's grasp of the French tongue. However, his meaning was clear.

'*Bordel de merde! Salope! Putain! Brûle en l'enfer!*' Closing his trousers, he headed for the door.

'I can lend you the jar,' Ophelia called after him. 'Benedict's Balsam is a Godsend—so many ailments for which it relieves unpleasant symptoms.'

Hardly had the Comte departed when there was another knock at the door. To Ophelia's surprise it was Hamish, who must have been lingering in the corridor. He didn't bother with any preliminaries and his tone was caustic.

'I thought I'd pay you a visit, but didn't realize there'd be a queue of gentleman callers.'

Ophelia refused to bite her tongue. 'You know as much about the psychology of women as you do of the mental state of Amazonian monkeys.'

'An apt comparison, I'm sure,' countered Hamish.

'If I choose to take a lover it will be my business, and none of yours. It's 1928, not 1828. I don't want to be someone else's idea of what a woman should be,' said Ophelia. 'And don't pretend you're some pinnacle of moral rectitude. Who knows how many women you've been sticking it to.' She was surprised at the invective in her voice. 'Besides which, it wasn't I who was practically engaged to someone else. Who were you thinking of while you were writhing on top of me?'

He had the decency, at least, to look away.

'Clearly, the night in the cabin meant nothing to you. As far as I can see, you couldn't get out of there quick enough.' Ophelia had been waiting too long to spew forth her resentment.

Hamish hung his head. 'You're right. It should never have happened. I gave a commitment to Felicité earlier this year. We said that we'd give it a go. I'm no saint, and nor is she...'

No, she's bloody not! thought Ophelia.

'...but I went too far with you... With the storm, and your ankle... our emotions ran away with us.' He continued, 'I'm travelling to Edinburgh in a few days. There's a position going at the Forestry Commission; the letter came yesterday, inviting me to speak with them.'

He hesitated, picking at a snagged piece of embroidery on the coverlet. 'If it works out, I'll lease a house in the city, for Felicité and I, and we'll make plans for the wedding.'

'Oh...' Ophelia realized that almost everything she'd wanted to say was no longer relevant. It would do her no good to be angry or resentful. The die had been cast.

She might be pregnant, or she might not, but she wouldn't use it to trap him. The thought of Hamish choosing her over Felicité simply because she might be carrying his child was abominable. It took great resolution, but Ophelia managed a small smile. She held out her hand for his.

'I wish you every happiness. I truly do.' She offered the customary shake of congratulation.

Hamish held onto her hand, placing his other on top as he looked her in the eye. 'She's the devil in a whirlwind. No idea if it'll work out, but I have to try.' He shrugged. 'She's got her past, just as I have mine, but we've agreed that it's a new start.'

Ophelia frowned. She wondered when the "new start" was beginning, or how much freedom Hamish was allowing Felicité. She'd heard of modern couples turning a blind eye to all manner of indiscretions and dalliances, pursuing their own private passions and whims, whilst maintaining the façade of marriage.

It seemed crass to ask outright if Hamish knew of Felicité's relationship with the Comte, not to mention McFinn. It wasn't her business.

Her hand still in his, she squeezed it gently. She'd been convinced that it was the hand hers had been waiting for.

The fury drained away as she looked into his face. 'Let's be friends.'

'Always,' said Hamish.

When he looked away, her chest tightened. Something precious, briefly shown to her, had been lost. Either that or she didn't yet have the knowledge to decipher the code.

21

SHOTS FIRED

The "Glorious Twelfth" arrived, the start of the grouse-shooting season. The twelfth day of August is perhaps the most anticipated of the year on the Scottish moors, when the two-legged assemble their guns to blast those of two wings from the sky.

The humble tenant farmers of Kintochlochie, as those before them through the centuries, send their sons to help in this bloody venture. Grouse must be driven into the path of waiting guns, and such work is delegated to those whose noses, and souls, are closest to the soil.

Like all ancient estates, Kintochlochie knows upon whom it should call when works needs to be done. Beat the birds from the moor, and load the guns, lads; it's your honour to serve.

By evening, hundreds of grouse would be strung up, destined for pastries and pies.

The shooting party set off after an early breakfast. Braveheart ran about, snuffling and chasing rabbits. Ophelia, though still stepping carefully upon her ankle, had spent far too long in her room, and was curious to see how the shoot was conducted. Rather than walking all the way, she'd be able to spend much of the time on the loaders' cart.

Pudding had been left behind with Morag, Constance, and most of the other ladies. She wasn't fond of loud noises; the first shot would send her scurrying for the nearest hiding place. Launcelot opted also to stay at the castle, wounded by the thought of the destruction of nature on such a scale.

The party, to include not only the Colonel and the Faucett-Plumblys (who were returning especially) but some of the neighbouring landowners, would convene by the loch for a lunch of cold meats, cheeses, and beer, before the guns went off again.

The Comte and his sister had clearly been shopping for their country visit. Their tweeds were the cleanest of all those gathered—the Comte in mustard and moss green, with a jaunty cap. Felicité's ensemble, in lilac and purple tones, matched the blooming heather. Her jacket nipped in delightfully at the waist, encircled by a belt, showing her figure to good effect.

'I had them cut it so,' Felicité told Ophelia, seeing her eyes upon the line. 'I prefer to show I am a woman. Some of today's clothes do not flatter. Comfort is not everything.'

Ophelia, wearing a long (and admittedly shapeless) coat of Morag's, in camouflaging brown, bit her tongue. She'd failed to bring adequate waterproof clothes with her, but there were plenty available for borrow at the castle. Morag had insisted that Ophelia don a hat with protective waxed coating.

Upon her head, Felicité was wearing the most adorable of felt cloches in deepest violet, adorned with green silk roses. Ophelia rather hoped it would rain. She wondered how chic Felicité would look with her hair hanging in rats' tails.

'I see ghastly Lady Faucett-Plumbly has returned to plague us,' commented Felicité, intentionally loud enough to be overheard. 'Have you noticed that her coiffure never moves?' Felicité was warming to her subject. 'I hear a rumour that she is bald, and relies on a clever wardrobe of wigs: one set rigidly, as now, to defy the weather; one cleverly indicating the need for a trip to the salon; another embellished with the hair of orphan children, which she wears to parties.'

'Goodness me!' Ophelia had not the least idea how to respond. She dared not look in the direction of the Faucett-Plumblys.

Hamish wandered over, giving Felicité a kiss upon the forehead and a warm smile for Ophelia.

'*Mon chéri*, we are discussing the feminine talent for artifice,' said Felicité.

'I hope,' said Hamish, 'that Ophelia may aspire to something rather more than that...'

Felicité shrugged.

In his wake the Comte sidled up, giving Ophelia's bottom an opportunistic squeeze. His eyes were glinting even more wickedly than usual, as if he'd started early on the whisky.

Receiving his gun from the loader, the Comte looked down the barrel and smirked. 'We shall see how I do. Perhaps, as in most things, I shall claim my target.'

Felicité kissed her step-brother's cheek. 'Of course, you shall be wonderful. Shoot well, and show the British that we too can murder nature's little creatures with a joyous heart.'

Ophelia rolled her eyes. As the fusillade began, the explosions were tremendous, echoing across the glen. Ophelia's ears were ringing.

Felicité covered hers. '*Mon Dieu!* We shall all be killed. It is most exhilarating!' Seized by some madness, she ran forward, to be met with much shouting.

'Get back, you ridiculous woman.'

'Keep in line there! You'll be shot, you know!'

She ducked down and sat on a rock, fearing to stir again.

The beaters, moving ahead through the moorland by the loch, drove the birds before them so that they flew upwards in all directions. The guns, placed in a line, each in their own semi-enclosed butt, then had their chance at blowing them from the sky.

By the end of the drive, a full twenty minutes of barbarism, the heather was strewn with corpses. The acrid smell of gunpowder hung heavy in the air, as every gun had unloaded a full two hundred cartridges.

'Ah!' exclaimed Felicité, seeing onlookers begin to collect the birds. 'The peasants are to receive their dinner. It is the kindness of your feudal system in action, is it not?'

Hardly likely, thought Ophelia.

'Hurry up, you men,' barked the Colonel. 'We've another drive to get in before lunch.'

Rex was busy doing his part, mouth stuffed with feathers, tail wagging proudly.

'How many have you bagged, Ebenezer?' yelled the Colonel. 'I'll warrant I've pulled in more than you and Hamish together.'

The sound of Ebenezer's teeth gnashing was palpable.

The Colonel was in his element. 'Seek hard, Rexy! Seek! Seek! And you, Faucett-Plumbly, don't think I didn't notice you bagging birds that should've been mine. Keep to your own bit of sky, you blaggard!'

Colonel Faversham's single eye seemed no impediment to the massacre of the poor grouse. However, the largest bag had been claimed by Lady Mildred Faucett-Plumbly, despite her being placed at the very end of the line. She'd been named by *The Field* as one of the best shots in the country three years running.

Meanwhile, Ophelia was pleased to see that Hamish's pile was modest.

'My Hamish. You are not the crack shot? Why are your birds so few and the old men have so many?' enquired Felicité, looking disappointed.

'Just not my day, darling,' he replied, hanging his grouse on the back of the cart.

'I think I'll head back,' said Ophelia. 'This really isn't my notion of a lark.'

'Do stay.' It was Hamish who'd spoken. He was at her elbow. 'It's not my idea of a good time either. Keep Felicité company, and out of harm's way for me? I'm worried she'll run forward again.'

'All right, but only one more drive. I'm not spending the whole day out here.'

A mist had begun rolling down through the southern part of the glen, so that only the castle towers remained visible, like a faery palace floating in the clouds.

Hamish lifted Ophelia onto the cart for the half-mile climb to a set of butts on the hillside. From there, they'd be looking down onto the birds as the beaters raised them from the moorland below.

Being higher up, the wind was stiff and had a distinct sharpness to it. The season was most certainly turning. Ophelia crouched behind the butt, seeking some protection.

The mist continued to creep, upwards now, like a ghostly spectre come to claim them. Its coolness entered Ophelia's lungs.

She could hear, more than see, the beaters down at the edge of the trees, thwacking the undergrowth to startle the birds.

With any luck, they'll miss most of their shots, thought Ophelia.

The fog allowed first no view at all, and then it shifted, giving sight of two-dozen grouse taking to the air.

'There are the blighters!' yelled the Colonel, and let off the first volley.

Ophelia could see that Hamish hadn't even bothered to raise his gun. Instead, partially cloaked by the thickness of the misted air, he was accepting a kiss from Felicité. She extended a delicate hand under the hem of Hamish's jacket.

That's it, thought Ophelia. *I'm not sitting here like a gooseberry.*

Marching out, she headed up the hill a little, knowing not to walk in front of the guns, and sat on the heather.

It was comfortable enough but too damp to sit for long.

Blast it! I'm going back, she decided. *I'll just go easy on the ankle. Slow but sure. I know these hills well enough to find my way.*

But she'd only gone twenty steps when another bank of fog rolled over, enveloping her, leaving her disoriented. She heard scuffling to her right. A hare darted out, looking her in the eye before scampering off.

She soon came to a rivulet flowing down into the loch. She was usually able to hop across but it had been raining the day before and was now too full for her to wade without making her feet sopping. Concentrating on following the stream down, knowing it would bring her out somewhere recognizable, Ophelia failed to notice that her path took her back towards the line of fire.

She soon heard the crack of guns—far nearer than she'd realized.

A bird dropped out of the sky and caught her unexpectedly on the elbow, making her cry out. She whirled around, sending her hat flying.

Suddenly, she seemed to be in the thick of it, grouse raining down on all sides, wings and breast bloodied by shot, eyes and beaks frozen open. One fluttered helplessly beside her, its last breath escaping its throat in a rasp, before surrendering to a broken neck.

Ophelia, frozen in terror, closed her eyes and shrieked. She was lost in a sea of mist and death.

'Hold the guns,' shouted a voice somewhere from within the chaos.

Moments passed, and then someone pushed Ophelia to the ground.

'You're safe. It's all right.' Hamish stroked her hair. 'Keep breathing, Ophelia. I've got you.'

She threw her arms around him, buried her head in his shoulder, and sobbed.

Most of the guns had ceased firing, but at least one person was still taking aim. Ophelia heard a high-pitched whistle through the air, as if a cluster of wasps had spun past at great speed. Something skimmed her cheek, hot, stinging.

Hamish tensed and swore. The outer shoulder of his jacket had been torn, and a small, red stain was seeping through.

'Damnation!' He gasped, clearly in pain. 'Hold your fire, dammit.'

Ophelia found her voice too. 'For God's sake, stop firing. Hamish has been hit!'

Her hands were shaking but she took her handkerchief from her pocket, found the injury and pressed the wadded fabric to it.

'It's not bad; only a flesh wound,' said Hamish, between gritted teeth.

'Eeee! My Hamish!' Felicité flew over the heather. 'Are you hurt? My love! I cannot bear it!'

Hamish stood as she reached them, enfolding her in his embrace, soothing her as, minutes before, he had Ophelia.

'Bloody stupid of me.' Ebenezer tottered down. 'Thought you were a deer in the mist... too carried away by the excitement of it all...' As Ebenezer drew closer and saw the blood upon Hamish's coat, he turned deathly pale.

'Good God, I could've killed you!' Ebenezer buckled at the knees and fell forward, muttering, 'Unforgiveable…unforgiveable!'

Ophelia ran to kneel beside him and as she rubbed the old man's shoulders, there came the familiar twist in her lower belly, and the slow sensation of wet warmth between her legs. Her monthly flow was several days late but had arrived at last. She realized how uptight she'd been, convincing herself that her single night with Hamish had left her with a baby.

It was a relief, of course, but a small part of her, further inside than she'd cared to look, sunk and died.

Braveheart stood on his hind legs to lick his injured master's face, and let forth a long, plaintive howl.

TAKING CHARGE

IT GAVE OPHELIA SOME PLEASURE TO KNOW THAT THE HAND LIFTED BY the Comte to his lips had fed liver and tripe to the dogs in the kitchen not half an hour before. She hoped the smell of offal was discernible.

'So we must go, my little rose. Hamish is to discuss the position of employment, which sounds most dire, and to see the surgeon in Edinburgh, though he is adamant his shoulder is without true harm. Meanwhile, I will take the sleeper to London, and onwards. The Mediterranean sun is calling to me.'

The family had gathered on the front steps to see off the party, Morag pressing a basket of homemade jams and pickles onto Felicité.

The Comte leaned in, so that only Ophelia would hear. 'Perhaps Felicité will join me soon—with Hamish, or perhaps not. He is a good man I believe, but that is not always enough. She likes to be under my thumb…and a very wicked, talented thumb it is.'

Ophelia glared and refrained from comment.

Braveheart, giving his own appraisal, raised his leg against that of the Comte.

Haddock and McFinn had almost finished loading up the car.

'Hamish, let us ask Ophelia what she thinks,' declared Felicité. Having convinced herself that Hamish's injury was minor, her tone had returned to one of mirth. 'Should my bear cut his beard? I think he should. I am scraped in places I cannot begin to mention.' Felicité laid a proprietorial hand upon Hamish's arm.

'Really, Felicité, some things are for behind closed doors!' said Hamish, looking uncomfortable.

Ophelia searched his eyes, seeking an answer to something else entirely. 'He should do as he likes,' she answered at last, as if returning from a long way off.

'As every man should,' added the Comte.

Felicité shook her head, laughing. 'You are too English, my dear, and too polite. My Hamish wishes to kiss me very much, and so often. The hair on his face pains me, and so it must go.'

Ophelia itched to slap her.

As the car drove off, Ophelia wondered if the next time she saw Hamish, he'd be a married man. Beneath her ribs, her heart surged in pain.

All the guests who'd stayed on at the castle after Morag's birthday celebrations had departed. Ranulph and Loretta were heading to London for a few weeks before returning across the Atlantic. Enid had been planning to stay on longer, but had instead accepted an invitation to join the Colonel on a tour of the Lake District, citing it as a wonderful opportunity for research.

'Wedding bells?' Morag had mused as they waved off the smiling pair.

'Hardly necessary at a certain age,' answered Constance. 'But I sense the Colonel is gallant. I predict a proposal by Christmas.'

Ophelia returned to former pastimes—playing cards with Constance and Morag, or backgammon with Ebenezer, and learning how to crochet, thanks to Constance.

Afternoon tea became a highlight, thanks to the easy chatter of the two older ladies. Ophelia grew accustomed to Morag's declaration that "few situations cannot be transformed by a strong cup of Earl Grey".

After her third, she would evoke her other belief, that "a buttered crumpet cheers even the most miserable".

How we do unite over simple comforts, thought Ophelia.

Lady Devonly would agree, and there would begin tales not only of living on beetles and bananas, but of utmost violence and degeneracy, set in the snake-swarmed jungles of Dahomey. A favourite anecdote involved cannibals offering marriage to the highly respectable married persons of Morag, or Constance, or to both together. The details seemed to grow more outrageous with each telling.

Ophelia would play for them, her fingers always seeming to choose Gershwin's *Man I Love* or *If I Had You*. Even her mother had approved of that one, since it was said to be a favourite of the Prince of Wales. She thought back to that evening, long ago, when Hamish had sat beside her on the stool, thumping out duets and laughing.

The kitchen, with its cheerful yellow enamelled stove, and its walls in bright buttermilk tones, drew her often. She'd chat with Mrs. Beesby, and could now make a tolerable scone.

Ophelia also began looking over the ledgers, discovering how income was generated and spent. She could see why Hamish had been focusing on the forestry potential of the glen. It was liable to prove more profitable than keeping livestock, although the highland cattle, with their long horns and flowing coats, remained a reliable source of funds.

From the library, she located various books on estate management. Many of the principles seemed like common sense; others Ophelia was familiar with, from having heard her father discussing their turkey farming in Norfolk. Ophelia began to feel that she could, perhaps make sense of it all.

She should write to her mother, explaining her grandmother's intention of bequeathing her the estate, but she kept putting it off.

Lady Finchingfield wouldn't be pleased at the way things had turned out. Far from feeling punished, Ophelia was content to have made her escape from London Society.

As to what came next, Ophelia was unsure, but the last thing she wanted was to provoke her mother into driving up and bundling Ophelia back to her old life.

In London, the many doors in the long corridor of her life had all been shut, but for two—one marked "marriage" and the other "spinsterhood". Neither had appealed to her under her mother's terms. Strangely, her time in Scotland was opening up doors; some led to places she was unsure she wished to venture, but she appreciated having the choice.

Morag and Constance would encourage her in whatever she chose to do next.

Ophelia didn't care what her mother thought. Her father, though a largely absent figure, was indulgent. He'd ensured a modest income for her since turning eighteen, and this would become more substantial when she reached twenty-five. She might do something interesting with it, if she had a mind to. She could invest in the estate, but there were other possibilities.

I might achieve anything really; do anything. Like Morag, I could head off on an expedition into the unknown. Well, perhaps not the unknown, but abroad. The world has so many treasures.

Ophelia also helped in the stables and, within a short while, became quite friendly with Lyle, who showed her things she'd never known about horses: how to brush them down properly and bathe them, how to clean and polish the tack, what to feed them (and not), even how to draw pus from a boil inside the hoof. It gave Ophelia satisfaction to think how horrified her mother would be.

She considered kissing Lyle, even though he was barely her own age, with a face as smooth as a baby's, but she soon realized that this would be folly. He was cordial company, nothing more. Soon afterwards, she heard from Mrs. Beesby that Una and Lyle were courting, and was glad that she hadn't interfered.

After the excitement of her mid-morning scamper, Pudding would retire to the rose-velvet chaise in the drawing room, her head nestled upon a plump cushion. In the midst of sweet snuffle-dreams, paws peddling as she chased imaginary rabbits down imaginary holes, her slumbers were as satisfying as her waking hours. Her memories of

London life were a mere shadow compared to the vibrancy of her Kintochlochie adventures.

Ophelia attempted to take the little terrier as her example.

She took out Esmeralda most days, though she couldn't help stopping often at the cabin. She hoped always, though without admitting it, to run into Hamish. Ophelia kept alive her secret wish for his unexpected return. Surely he might yet throw in his ambitions with the Forestry Commission, choosing instead to spend his life at Kintochlochie.

It seemed so long ago that she'd fantasized of taking a host of lovers. Ophelia knew her soul a little better now, including a few of its secret caves.

The solemn beauty of the estate, increasingly, gave her fortitude and a sense of contentment—the loch, reflecting the ethereal depth of the sky and the grass shivering in the wind.

With each passing day her eyes, though wistful, became brighter and her cheeks rosier. Ophelia could walk or ride for hours now without becoming tired, the landscape invigorating her.

She explored the tranquility of the lower slopes of the purple-heathered hills, all the while gazing up at the more brutal peaks.

Ophelia had come to hold dear the murmuring streams and the rugged mountains, towering on all sides, watching over the castle.

Like Amelia Earhart, Ophelia had often dreamt of learning to fly. Perhaps she wasn't quite brave enough to fly across the Atlantic, but she longed to soar with a feeling of freedom.

She'd watched the eagles sweep overhead, circling and scanning for rabbits in the heather, thinking how majestic and self-contained they were, necks outstretched, powerful in their independence. Wouldn't it be wonderful if she might be the same?

If she swam out into the loch, the water might dissolve away the layers so carefully cultivated by her mother and her London life, and she'd discover what lay underneath.

~

As she was drawing her bath one evening, there was a knock upon the door. It was Morag, carrying her granddaughter's tray of cocoa, with a cup also for herself. She beckoned for them to sit upon the bed together.

'I received a letter from your mother, Ophelia,' began Lady MacKintosh. 'She wishes for you to return to London, although the season is over, of course. She writes that the Earl of Woldershire, young Percival, is yet to make a proposal to any other debutante, and that she believes he would take you if, as she puts it, you've "gained your senses". How would you like me to reply?'

Ophelia shrugged. 'I've been having a dream lately where I'm in a beautiful garden, but hemmed in on all sides by a tall brick wall. It's covered in tumbling wisteria, honeysuckle and roses, and the scent is overpowering. I search for the door but there is none, so I try to climb the roses, to find some way over. I keep trying, but always slip back.'

She omitted to add that, sometimes, there were imaginary children running through the garden (in her mind's eye, they all had curling auburn locks).

Morag patted her hand. 'Go on, Ophelia.'

'I thought that the only reason I didn't want to marry Percival was because I wasn't attracted.' Ophelia blushed. 'He didn't make my toes tingle, Granny...'

'Say no more,' Morag declared. 'I know just how important that side of marriage is, my dear.'

Ophelia searched for the words she needed. 'I realize now that it was more than that. I know that most women are content with a comfortable family life, a good income and a modicum of social status. Percival was offering all that, and more, but whenever I think of being married to him, or to anyone from that set, it's like reaching the final pages of a book, and realizing that there won't be any more pages to come, just that final ending of apparent "happiness", over and over, forever, without any real surprises.'

She took a sip of her cocoa. 'There are so many adventures yet to be had, but I don't think I'll have any of them if I marry Percival, or anyone like him.'

Pudding, lying beside them on the quilt, shifted into her favourite pose—legs splayed, revealing the softest white hair of her underside. Ophelia absent-mindedly stroked the fondant pink of her belly.

Ophelia continued, 'It's as if I'm yearning for something, but I'm unsure of what. Some days, I feel as trapped as I ever did in London, with no sense of where I want to flee to, but knowing that I can't remain as I am. Something has to change.'

It was such a relief to finally be speaking her mind, letting someone else hear her worries and the resentments she'd been carrying. 'Have you noticed how many men spend time telling us their opinions, even on things they know little about, rather than asking us ours? And yet I can never work out what men are really thinking.'

'Why should you! Why not spend time deciding what you're thinking instead?' said Morag.

Ophelia gave her grandmother's hand a squeeze. 'I sometimes think how wonderful it might be to wake up in the morning and find that I *was* a man. I'd be able to do as I liked, and be valued for what I say, and what I do, rather than for how I look, or who I was married to.'

'I felt just the same as a young woman. It was worse back then. Most of us didn't receive any sort of education, and you were pitied if you hadn't found a husband by the age of twenty-one. But when I met Angus, I saw that he was my soul mate.' Morag smiled, recalling happy times. 'He wanted me to experience everything alongside him. I had no idea what lay in store when we travelled to West Africa, but I knew he'd always have my interests at heart. We discovered it all together.'

Ophelia drained the last from her cup. 'I think I've spent far too much time letting things happen to me rather than making things happen.'

23

NIGHT DREAMS

OPHELIA SAT ON THE BATH'S EDGE, SENDING HER REGULAR PRAYER OF thanks to her grandmother for having installed the latest in plumbing technologies. The boiler heaved a little and the hot water spluttered into the huge ceramic tub, but the pressure was good and it wasn't long before she was relaxing in the warmth.

Her mind drifted, as it so often did, to Hamish, and to the night they'd spent at the cabin. The aroma of his body and the roughness of his beard. The press of his mouth, and his tongue! Her fingers crept downwards, beneath the surface of the water. Ophelia had been sent away to repent her sins and had instead tumbled from one escapade to another.

No doubt, Lady Finchingfield would say she'd been 'violated' but, even with the way things had turned out, she wouldn't change any of it.

She sighed, her pulse quickening as she pressed her hand lower, and thought of Hamish...

By the time she'd finished, the water had gone quite cold.

~

Unable to sleep, Ophelia kept the fire burning and sat late into the night, into its still, dark hours, wondering about the other young women who'd lived in the castle over the centuries. Who had slept in her room and poked the embers in the grate, seeking their warmth and comfort as she did. She saw them, as if sitting beside her, in the dim glow of the dying flames.

Ophelia rose, put on her robe, and stared out into the ink blue of the night, following the moon's glimmer on the water.

How long had she spent looking into the depths of the loch, as if into the deeper reaches of herself? Something was down there, waiting to be brought to the surface.

~

On the rooftop, an owl was watching, wide-eyed. Beneath its wing, the castle sat quiet.

Maggie, snoring, dreamt she was wearing a neat little tearoom uniform, dishing out fondant fancies with silver tongs.

Jennet turned in her sleep, eyebrows knitted. In her dreams, there was endless glassware to wash and no one to help.

Una lay restless, her toes itching for something she couldn't quite imagine.

Haddock was sound in his slumbers, cycling the country lanes of his youth. A girl rode beside him, gingham skirts flapping, hair loose in the wind.

Nessa's fancy took her to a cottage in which she was stoking the fire, a baby playing on the rug and a husband smoking his pipe at the table.

McFinn dreamt of the woods, deep in velvet enticements.

Mrs. Beesby was still awake. Her feet had been aching.

I'm getting too old for this lark, she thought. *Perhaps I ought to open a little bed and breakfast in Edinburgh.*

But she'd never leave. How could she? She'd stay until Lady Morag didn't need her anymore.

A rat scurried from the reeds by the loch's edge, and the owl swooped silently to claim its prize.

24

A SMALL BEGINNING

It was in her newly contented, if not yet truly happy, state of mind that Ophelia set out for a walk around the loch with Pudding, on one of the last, muted-golden afternoons of late summer.

There is always a faintly melancholy air about those last days of warmth, when birds are already contemplating their flight to more temperate climes. Ophelia felt the stirrings of change; that this season was ending and another was about to begin.

The broderie anglaise hem of her white cotton frock was slightly torn and coming unravelled. She ought to put the dress, worn soft from wear, aside. Still, it was good enough for a ramble.

Having passed through the trees on the eastern bank of the loch, she emerged into the sun and, there, what awaited her...?

A view more wondrous than sun-dappled water or the solemn glitter of the stars. She saw the muscular shoulders and curve of a man's naked back, his thighs, and firm buttocks—a man entirely stripped, ready to take a swim.

A feast for any woman's eyes but for hers especially, for who should that man be but Hamish, returned at last.

She watched him wade in, until his lower half was decently submerged.

She wanted to be honest, to lay her heart bare. If she spoke her mind, wouldn't everything become real, and solid and reliable. She could let love wrap her up utterly, just as she'd let Kintochlochie claim her. Ophelia belonged to the glen, and to the castle which would one day belong to her.

She settled upon shouting, 'I see you're back.'

The startled look upon his face, his head twisting to see who'd called out, brought a smile to hers. In turning, he showed her the width of his chest, the smoothness of his lower abdomen, and the depth of his pelvic muscles. The damage to his shoulder seemed to have healed well, leaving little more than a pale scar. Ophelia took in the contours of that glorious body and he stood, silent, allowing her to do so.

He said nothing but, after some moments began to move, slowly and purposefully, back towards the bank into shallower water. He revealed, inch by tantalizing inch, the last portion of his lower torso, leading into thick, auburn hair, and the solidity of his meat, well-girthed. He planted his legs boldly and folded his arms upon his chest. Ophelia could have sworn that he'd angled his pelvis forward, defying her not to look, as if saying: "Here it is; admire all you like!"

The smile he gave her reached back into the forest shade, and the granite crags above. Such smiles have men always given women.

A flood of heat threatened to overwhelm her. Her body remembered everything.

Letting him see where her eyes lingered, she said, 'Is Felicité back too?'

A shadow flitted across his face. 'I thought she might consider staying in Scotland, but it appears I'm not a good judge of women.' He hesitated. 'What I'm offering isn't enough to tempt her, although she did sample at her leisure,' said Hamish wryly. 'I woke one morning to find a note from her, saying she'd gone to join Ranulph in London, with plans to launch herself on Hollywood. She's in no haste to wed, or so I believe.'

'In some ways that's very sensible of her,' admitted Ophelia, with a sudden surge of happiness. She wriggled her toes, feeling that she'd like to kick off her shoes.

She added, 'The "not-rushing-into-marriage" part and planning to enjoy herself; of that, I must confess I approve.'

'You'll soon be off then, I take it? The Comte has returned to residence in his villa on the Riviera; he tells me you're always welcome,' Hamish added archly.

His arms remained folded across his chest, but he made no move to cover his manhood.

'That's tempting,' she answered, unable to resist the mischief of it. 'However, I've become rather devoted to the glen, and the loch, and to the mountains. Nature has its charms.'

Hamish's eyes held her fast, filled not only with desire but with tenderness, and something else she thought she recognized.

She paused, wondering how much to tell Hamish.

'It's more than that though,' she began. 'I feel a responsibility to the estate. I'm part of its future now. Morag is bequeathing Kintochlochie to me. I've also grown very fond of everyone...even Ebenezer.'

In the long silence between them she felt his uncertainty. At last, he spoke.

'Could you be fond of me?'

In answer, she stepped out of her shoes, rolled down her stockings and tucked up her dress, leaving her legs bare, feeling Hamish's eyes upon their length. Leaving Pudding on the bank, she paddled out, through the reeds, almost losing her balance in the slippery mud.

She put down her hands to steady herself then pushed a lock of hair from her face, unaware that she'd left a streak of pondweed slime. She advanced, carefully, through the water, until she almost faced him.

It was as if she were remembering something she had lived before, that had left her softly drowsy and contented. Ophelia felt a strange happiness—one she could not bear to articulate, in case it might slip away.

She cast down her eyes, fearful suddenly of meeting his, willing her heart to calm itself. When she raised them, she found that Hamish had moved considerably closer and had lowered his face to hers. He licked his thumb, gently wiping away the smear on her cheek.

'Why is it that you only want to kiss me when I'm covered in filth?' she asked.

He took that as an invitation.

~

What next for Hamish and Ophelia?
Read on to find out... in 'Highland Christmas'

IF YOU'VE ENJOYED 'HIGHLAND PURSUITS'

READ ON...

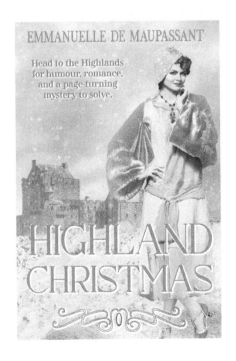

A ghostly presence is haunting Castle Kintochlochie.
Amidst preparations for the festive season, a malevolent force stalks
the ancient corridors. Could Lady Ophelia's life be in danger?

... and, don't miss the wonderful third volume of the trilogy: 'Highland Wedding'.

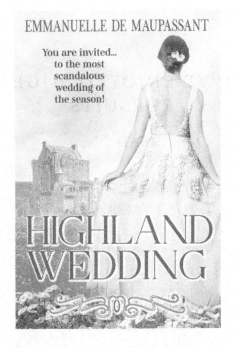

A SNEAK PEEK...

FROM 'HIGHLAND CHRISTMAS'

The mountains surrounding Castle Kintochlochie were well-frosted, but the fire was blazing cosily in the drawing room as Lady Morag MacKintoch took afternoon tea, seated with her granddaughter Ophelia and long-time companion Lady Constance Devonly.

'Oh, how marvellous!' exclaimed Morag, looking up from the letter in her hands. 'Constance! Ophelia! Our old friend the Colonel has proposed to dearest Enid, and she's consented to take him! It's like something from one of Enid's novels, except for the heroine being a little more mature in years.'

'Goodness me! That was quick work,' said Ophelia, licking sugar from her fingers and reaching to receive the pink notepaper from her grandmother.

'Delightfully romantic,' remarked Constance, taking a sip of tea. 'They were rather love-struck when they set off together for their jaunt to the Lake District after your lovely sixtieth birthday party, Morag. I did wonder if something of the kind might happen.'

Morag contemplated the array of cakes on the stand. 'About time he settled down. He and Enid seem very well suited.'

'Jolly good luck to them, I say.' Ophelia scanned through Enid's correspondence, tucking a curl of her unruly, dark hair behind her ear.

'Never too late for love, even for an old cavalier like the Colonel. Although I do think it's rather rum that they're cavorting about the Lake District, getting up to all sorts. No one would approve of me behaving like that!'

'I know, dearest. I don't suppose the world approves terribly of Enid either, but she's old enough for certain things to go less remarked upon.' Morag reached for an iced fancy. 'Nevertheless, I expect Colonel Faversham has been signing them in as Colonel and Missus, to avoid raising eyebrows.'

'Easy enough to find a ring to pretend with, I suppose,' said Ophelia.

'Yes, dearest.' Lady MacKintoch fed a cake crumb to Aphrodite, her beloved Pekinese, who was perched in her lap.

Ophelia's own little terrier, Pudding, was sitting at her feet, licking her lips, eager for a similar treat. However, Ophelia never allowed her sugar; bad for the teeth, and Pudding was excitable enough as it was.

'Will they be heading off to Gretna Green, like eloping lovers, do you think?' asked Ophelia, tearing the crust from a cucumber sandwich and passing it to the dainty lips of Pudding.

'Oh no, darling. Did you not read to the end? Enid asks if they might be married from the chapel, here at Castle Kintochlochie.'

Aphrodite shifted in her mistress' lap, her nose twitching at the scent of almonds in anticipation of another morsel.

'Neither has many relations to speak of,' sighed Morag, 'Their parents are gone, and the Colonel's only brother was killed in the Boer War, before he managed to have children. Enid's sister Prudence may make the journey; her other sibling succumbed to the Spanish flu, years ago.'

She leaned over to squeeze Lady Devonly's arm. 'As did Constance's own dear child. Such a terrible illness. No one was safe.'

Constance looked to the window and hid her face in her teacup for a few moments.

'Enid suggests a small party, but I'm sure we can do better,' mused Morag. 'I've already written to your mother, Ophelia, to suggest she and your father join us. It's been far too long since Daphne visited the estate and she must be missing you, darling.'

Ophelia forced a smile. It had been rather blissful not to have her mother about. Moreover, Lady Finchingfield might resume in her persistence to see her daughter married. Scotland was suiting Ophelia perfectly well, and she'd no desire to return to London, to be promenaded like a prize cow before a paddock of panting bulls.

'We had such a splendid time at my birthday celebration,' continued Morag. 'We might recreate the festivities of the summer. Since it was that event which brought the Colonel and Enid together, it would seem apt.'

'What a super idea!' Constance pressed Morag to take the last of the macaroons. 'I know the Beltons and Faucett-Plumblys are travelling up soon.'

'Utterly bliss-making,' said Ophelia, her teeth clenching at the thought. She'd spent a large part of Morag's party avoiding unwanted attention and had gotten herself in a shameful pickle not long afterwards with young Peregrine Belton. She blushed to think of how she'd attempted to seduce him when they were out in his car, and how he'd dumped her, unceremoniously, upon the doorstep of Castle Kintochlochie. Peregrine had scarcely been able to escape fast enough.

'That's settled then.' Lady MacKintoch beamed. 'Constance, didn't you mention that Felicité is soon returning…from America, isn't it, with her new husband? Wouldn't it be fun to invite them? We need some youthful glamour to offset all the ancient bones.'

Ophelia's fingers tightened on her cup.

'Jolly good thinking,' said Lady Devonly, rising to give the fire a poke. 'When does Enid want us to plan for, Morag dear?'

'She's suggested a Christmas wedding,' replied Lady MacKintoch, popping a stray raspberry into her mouth. 'Isn't it exciting!'

ABOUT THE AUTHOR

Emmanuelle lives in the Highlands of Scotland with her husband
(maker of tea and fruit cake) and her snuffle snoof, Archie, her
favourite hairy pudding connoisseur of squeaky toys and bacon treats.

www.emmanuelledemaupassant.com

ALSO BY
EMMANUELLE DE MAUPASSANT

Discover 'The Lady's Guide' series: historical romance brimming with adventure, mystery and intrigue

The Lady's Guide to Scandal

The Lady's Guide to a Highlander's Heart

The Lady's Guide to Mistletoe and Mayhem

The Lady's Guide to Escaping Cannibals

The Lady's Guide to Deception and Desire

The Lady's Guide to Tempting a Transylvanian Count

Each can be read individually and in any order.

AN INVITATION

If you love Facebook, come and join the 'Historical Harlots' reader group.
Very relaxed, lots of fun, and everyone is welcome.

Made in the USA
Monee, IL
14 June 2024

59862483R00105